SWEET 15

Emily
Adler &
Alex
Echevarria

Marshall Cavendish

This book is for Mom and Allan.

*It takes many players to raise the curtain on a book. We would like to
thank the following curtain raisers: Caren Johnson, our beloved agent,
Barrie Allen, our high school BFF, and Robin Benjamin,
our magical editor at Marshall Cavendish.
Thank you, players! Play on!*
—Emily and Alex

Marshall Cavendish Corporation
99 White Plains Road
Tarrytown, NY 10591
www.marshallcavendish.us/kids

This book is a work of fiction. Names, characters, places, and incidents are products
of the author's imagination and are used fictitiously. Any resemblance to actual events
or locales or persons, living or dead, is entirely coincidental.

Library of Congress Cataloging-in-Publication Data
Adler, Emily.
Sweet 15 / by Emily Adler and Alex Echevarria. — 1st ed.
p. cm.
Summary: Shortly before her fifteenth birthday, Destiny Lozada's traditional Puerto
Rican mother and feminist older sister hijack her *quinceañera*, each pushing her own
agenda and ignoring the possibility that Destiny, a skateboarding tomboy, might have
her own ideas about the coming-of-age ritual she is about to participate in.
ISBN 978-0-7614-5584-4
[1. Individuality—Fiction. 2. quinceañera (Social custom)—Fiction. 3.
Puerto Ricans—New York (State)—New York—Fiction. 4. Family life—New York
(State)—New York—Fiction. 5. Interpersonal relations—Fiction. 6.
Schools—Fiction.] I. Echevarria, Alex. II. Title. III. Title: Sweet fifteen.
PZ7.A26154Sw 2009
[Fic]—dc22
2008021391

Book design by Anahid Hamparian
Editor: Robin Benjamin

Printed in China (E)
First edition
10 9 8 7 6 5 4 3 2 1

mc Marshall Cavendish

ACT ONE

"What? You, too? I thought I was the only one."
—C. S. Lewis, from *The Four Loves*,
chapter IV on "Friendship"

FAMILY

Here's how it went down, the beginning of The End. Breakfast: out of the blue, my mom, in a red bathrobe, with her makeup already on, making coffee in our big yellow kitchen, hit me over the head with "Destiny is having a *quinceañera*!"

"No way!" shouted my sister, America, who was setting the table with me. "Papi!"

Butter sizzled on heated pans. I looked over at my father, tall and straight in his white dress shirt, black slacks, and dark shoes. His eyes were fixed on the eggs he was preparing. He was trying his best to stay out of it. My poor Papi. He knew what was coming.

It's a running joke in our family that my parents have a mixed marriage, even though they're both Puerto Rican: my mother roots for the Mets, while my father, like me, is a Yankees fan. People always say I take after my dad, sort of quiet, you know? Watching, waiting, not getting crazy. We even look alike. We're both tall and thin and have the same dark brown hair and eyes.

"I'm cooking," my father complained and added green and red peppers, tomatoes, diced onions, and mushrooms to his omelet.

5

"Anyway," said America, "it's not going to happen, Mami!"

"It isn't your decision," said my mother.

I flung myself down at the table. I was wearing my pajama top and shorts and flip-flops, still sweaty from sleep.

"You can't!" America shouted again, waving her arms. "You can't force Destiny to stuff herself into a clown dress and have a *quinceañera*!"

Fact check: a *quinceañera* (which is Spanish for "fifteen years") is like a Sweet Sixteen party or bat mitzvah, only the Spanish, or Mexican, or Puerto Rican, or Cuban, or Central or South American version for fifteen-year-old girls, with chunks of religious and cultural stuff mixed together. The *Q* girl is escorted into the party by an escort called a *caballero*, followed by her own "court" (like she's a queen, if you can believe it), which includes a group of seven girls called *damas* and seven guys called *chambelanes*. (Usually, it's up to the *Q* girl to ask a boy to be her *caballero*. Ack!) They all have to enter together and do this waltz at the start of the party. It's basically a fancy birthday party, but it looks a lot like a wedding. My fifteenth birthday was only three months away: October 28th.

My mom tried to rope my sister into having a *quinceañera*, but gave up when America went on a hunger strike to protest the oppression of young girls around the world who are forced to wear pouffy dresses and fake diamond tiaras. My mom never noticed the disappearing leftovers or the fact that America actually gained five pounds during her supposed hunger strike.

"Destiny's my daughter," my mother pronounced and pressed the brew button on the coffeemaker.

6

"She's my little sister," America declared and stared defiantly at my mom, hands on her hips.

While they had their standoff, I squinted at the TV in the living room and tried to make it turn on using mind control. I love TV. I watch it every day. Mostly *South Park* and *Family Guy* and baseball and stuff on PBS and *Animal Planet* and, okay, I admit it, sometimes *My Super Sweet 16* on MTV. There's something for everybody.

I don't trust people who don't watch TV.

"Destiny is NOT having a *quinceañera*!" my sister proclaimed and opened the cupboard door above my mother's head. "A *quince* stands for virginity, chastity, and nonsense. It's a rehearsal for how to walk, talk, sit, eat, and obey. We don't need any of that. It's also used to show wealth. And we don't *have* any of that."

I glanced up at my sister in her tight jeans and Wonder Woman T-shirt. America is not fat or skinny; she's big boned and strong with curves and a natural tan. A lot like my mom. I think that's why they fight so much—they're a lot alike, but they don't realize it. America's hair is black and wild like my mom's used to be before she went blonde (with some help).

My sister is a senior this year and wants to be a lawyer. She's wanted that ever since she read *To Kill a Mockingbird* when she was ten. Me? I'm totally clueless about my future. Although, I've worried a lot lately about growing too tall for my age (I'm almost five-feet-eight) and that my legs seem too long for the rest of me.

"The *quinceañera* is simply a birthday party for family and friends," said my mother.

"Well," my sister replied, "I'm not going!"

"What is the *problema*?" my father asked, finally turning from the stove. He brushed his mustache and brown goatee with his fingertips, which is something he does when his calm is broken.

"Your daughter," said my mother, pouring coffee into two blue mugs. "The bad one. She's trying to destroy poor Destiny's *quinceañera*. She's acting like I'm sending Destiny to prison."

"You might as well be," said America. "*Quinceañera* is just another tool used by The Man to imprison women in a lifelong sentence of loveless marriages filled with dirty dishes and ungrateful babies and dirty babies and ungrateful dishes!"

"A *quinceañera*," said my mom, adjusting her red-framed glasses, "is a beautiful religious ceremony."

America shook her head. "Please. The only time you go to church is to play Bingo."

"*Eso no es verdad*," my mom protested.

Although it is kind of true. My mom likes to think she's super religious out of respect for her own parents who were strict Catholics. But she's not.

"We can't afford some huge *quince*," said America, sitting down next to me. "The only reason you're remotely interested all of a sudden, Mami, is because Mrs. Hernandez just had one, and you're jealous and trying to prove something."

Which might also be true.

Mrs. Hernandez is R-I-C-H.

My parents are not.

Last month Mrs. H threw a huge *quinceañera* for her

daughter, Yasmin, and we all went.

"If Destiny went through with your *quince* idea," my sister continued, staring at me, "she would be doing it because she doesn't want to hurt your feelings, not because she's some totally unoriginal, goody-two-shoes follower!"

Now *that's* true. I am original. I am *not* a goody-two-shoes follower.

Up until then, I'd been happy to stay out of it. My dad had already gone back to the safety of his stove. We know when we're beat. But maybe . . . if I said something . . .

"I think—"

My sister patted my head like she was handling everything fine without my help, and my mother put up a hushing finger and said, "Don't let America upset you."

"Me?" said America. "What about you!"

And people wonder why my dad and I are so quiet? I didn't try again. I wasn't looking for trouble even if trouble was looking for me. I would just think about TV and our cat, Natasha, who'd been lying on the kitchen counter, licking herself, which is totally nasty but natural, I guess. America's voice had gotten so loud that Natasha stopped licking and stared up at her as if to say, "Can't you see I'm workin' here?" Natasha's so smart. Any day now she'll start talking. Hopefully she won't only talk about what it's like to be licking yourself all day long. (Whoa, *chica*. Too much information. Catnip, anyone?)

My sister took over again, making her case. "You guys raised us to speak more English than Spanish. So that we'd do well in school and be successful and have all the things you never had. And that's what we're doing."

America and I go to this private school, Columbus Prep, despite the fact that we're not rich. I'm one of those fourteen-year-old scholarship girls who live in Manhattan on West 97th Street in a rent-stabilized apartment. You know, the kind you see on *Gossip Girl*. NOT.

"And this is how you repay us for living out your dream?" America went on. "By yanking us back a few hundred centuries? What's next? Maybe Destiny should get married at fifteen and pop out babies. Would that make you happy?"

"Don't say: pop out babies." My mother pushed back her dyed blonde hair and made a sour face, as if she didn't hear the rest of the argument.

America retaliated. "Pop out. Pop out. Pop out!"

Between you and me, I'm not popping out anything anytime soon. And if a baby ever wants to come out of me, it will have to do it alone with no help from me. Just creep out slowly when my back is turned and shut off the lights when you go. If I want pain and drama, I'll go window-shopping on 5th Avenue with my sister and my mom.

"Popping out babies is not an achievement," shouted America. "Cockroaches have babies!"

My mother gasped, her jaw nearly touching the edge of the counter. "Did you just call your mother a cockroach?" Then she turned to my father at the stove. "Jon?"

I knew that tone. It meant that she wanted a response *pronto*. But my poor father wanted no part of it. He only shrugged, said, *un momento*, and focused harder on his eggs, which must have been cooked to a crisp by now.

"No *momento*!" America slammed her fist on the table. "Papi, you can't let Mami do this!"

My dad smoothed back his mustache and muttered something about what is he supposed to do, he just lives here.

"Okay, fine," said my sister. "But we're not giving up without a good old family fight. Right, Dusty?"

Dusty is America's nickname for me. I like when she uses it. I call her Merry.

But fight? What fight? I'll take eggs, toast, butter, home fries, this week's *TV Guide*, and a brand-new Plan B skateboard for my birthday, hold the fight, please.

"Leave her alone." My mother smiled at me sweetly. "Don't let your *hermana* bully you."

My sister looked at my mother like she had *loca* stamped on her forehead. "What about you?"

"Me? I want whatever will make my daughters happy."

That was the last straw. America lunged across the kitchen table and STABBED MY MOTHER WITH A FORK!

Really? Nah.

She did, however, jump up and grab a small bottle of apple juice from the fridge, gather her iPod and messenger bag (splattered with two thousand five hundred SAFE SEX and WEAR CONDOMS buttons), and try to storm out of our apartment, saying that she wasn't hungry anymore, which for my parents was almost as bad as being stabbed with a fork.

"No more fighting," announced my mother, stopping America in her tracks. "Let's all sit down and have our breakfast, *por favor*."

My sister dropped her bag, sighed deeply, and sat down next to my mom.

My mother pulled America close and kissed her face over and over. My sister did not resist.

"Are we still going shopping tomorrow?" my mom asked.

"Yes," said America, munching on some toast. "But I'm not talking to you."

My mom plucked a red rose from the vase on the table and put it behind my sister's ear.

"Stop!" America laughed.

I swear they're both *locas*. But the truth is that America and my mother are really close in their own way. I guess I envy how close they are sometimes.

"Why are you so stubborn?" asked my mother.

"I won't even justify that with a reply," America said. "Right, Papi?"

"Right," said my father as he brought over a hot platter of eggs and home fries. He sat next to me.

"What? Are you agreeing with this lunatic?" asked my mother.

"Who me? Am I agreeing with this lunatic, Destiny?"

"No," I said as he handed me the ketchup. "You're just being Papi."

"I'm just being me," my father told my mother and grabbed his blue coffee mug. "You didn't put too many scoops in the coffee, did you, honey?"

"If I want to drink the brown water you call coffee, dear," said my mom, "I'll boil dirt."

She leaned over and kissed his cheek. Whatever the coffee

tastes like, they love to drink it all day long. (Their blood is 75 percent Juan Valdez. Somebody call for an intervention.)

We ate breakfast while my mom went on and on about Puerto Rican culture this, Puerto Rican families that, Puerto Rican women are, if you're Puerto Rican then, blah, blah. My parents grew up together in Isabela, Puerto Rico. They were high-school sweethearts and got married and moved here right after graduation. America and I have never even been to P.R.

I knew that if I said yes to a *quince*, for the next three months, my sister and my mother would be fighting like snakes on a plane, while my father and I would hide out in our rooms. I felt as if they weren't thinking about me at all; they were using my *quinceañera* as another excuse to go at each other, which is really their favorite sport. But I never say anything to America or my mother about how their fighting makes me feel. I don't want to make things worse.

"How do you feel about this *quinceañera*, Destiny?" my father asked, as if my opinion actually counted.

"I don't know." I leaned my head on his shoulder.

Like I said, I'm just your average fourteen-year-old Puerto Rican-American girl, a soon-to-be-ninth grader with legs too freakishly long for her body, trying to survive *mi familia*.

5 weeks later: september

OMAR AND NICOLAS

It's the last day before school starts, and I want it to be a good one. After breakfast, I shower and dress, grab my skateboard, tuck my hair under a Yankees cap, and head for the door. I'm sneaking out before my mother, who is in her bedroom getting dressed for work, catches me and begins yapping in fast Spanish about making appointments, preparing speeches, and getting the *quince* invitations ready.

Yeah. I totally caved.

I also promised America (who is NOT coming to my Sweet Fifteen but assures me we'll have our own little birthday celebration) that I won't have a *caballero,* basically to avoid WWIII. My sister argued that I don't have a boyfriend so why have a phony date or a fake escort or whatever you call it, to guide me into my own party like a show pony, as if he owns me, as if I don't have two strong female legs to do it myself?

Whatever.

I have some of my *damas* already: my best friends, Stephanie and Erin. Five more to go.

I have only one *chambelán* so far: my buddy Omar. Six more to go.

Whatever.

I make it outside my apartment. But as I get to the elevator, I hear my front door open behind me and footsteps heading my way. Oh no! I turn and there's my dad (thank God) approaching in his usual white shirt, black slacks, dark shoes, and black doorman's jacket, heading off to his job. (I hate his uniform. It makes him look like an undertaker.)

My father and I wait for the elevator, which takes forever as always. He smiles at me. I smile back. We're quiet until the elevator arrives and we get in.

"Floor?" my father asks, all professional.

"First floor, please, Mr. Lozada."

"Your wish is my command."

The moment we step into the lobby, the building manager comes out of his ground-floor apartment like he was waiting for us.

"Jon!" he calls out in his thick Russian accent. "I get call from office today."

My father holds out his hand. "I'm on it, Iggy. Don't you worry."

Iggy shakes my father's hand, but his eyes are worried. "You don't pay rent on time, they make problem for me, Jon. I don't need no problem."

My father nods and answers quickly, "I understand. No problem."

"Big problem, Jon, I telling you."

Big problem? Oh, no. As if things weren't bad enough.

"See you tonight, honey," my dad says to me. He kisses my forehead and hurries out the door.

Iggy mutters and walks off. I stand there alone in the

lobby. Can we not afford to pay the rent? That's never happened before. It's like I've stepped into another world. All I need now is to discover that I'm adopted and my parents in New Jersey want me back. (New Jersey? Fuggedaboutit!) My parents aren't irresponsible; they must be overwhelmed with all this *quince* stuff. They usually pay everything ahead of time. My mother handles the bills, because she's better with the practical and financial sides of things. In the last five weeks, she's done the work of one year and put deposits down on a church and a reception hall, a photographer, AND a *quinceañera* dress from a place called La Bridal on East 110th Street. It's a deep, dark emerald green dress and amazingly, not completely hideous. I can half-picture myself wearing it.

But I feel guilty. I know my parents can't really afford all of this, and every day for the past five weeks I've thought about bringing up the whole money thing. And then I chicken out. I don't want my parents to feel bad. I could get a part-time job and help pay for it, but I know my dad wouldn't let me. He doesn't want us working during the school year.

School hasn't even started yet and already I need another vacation.

I leave the building and hop on my skateboard. I roll along 97th Street toward the sunshine and green trees of Central Park West, where Omar is waiting on the corner.

Omar is absolutely my oldest and best male buddy. He lives alone with his mom (who is also friends with my mom) and grew up in the housing project three blocks from my building. We had such good times together when we were little kids. We're still inseparable during the summer, and during the school year we sometimes study together. Omar's a bit of a braniac. He goes to Brandeis on West 84th, a public school. But he knows my situation, and he understands what it's like when your family doesn't have a lot of money and you're surrounded by people who do.

Omar's my go-to-guy. Last summer when our cable broke down and my dad took a while to fix it, I was going through withdrawal, shaking and vomiting and everything. The doctors had given up hope for me. (Don't you understand? I was going to die from withdrawal!) Man, I had to get over to Omar's to watch TV, quick! I eased back into it slow, first with *Family Guy*—easy Destiny, small sips—until I was ready for the strong stuff, some full-blown MTV and some reality-show action. See, Omar saved my life!

We used to go skateboarding every Sunday with a couple of other boys from the neighborhood. But lately, the other guys tease me, saying idiotic stuff like, "Hey, the letters on your 'Vote for Pedro' T-shirt are totally getting stretched out!" Real original.

I liked it when all of us could just have fun, racing on the bike path in Central Park under the trees, the wind whistling in my ears. Now I skateboard only with Omar, because he hardly ever notices I'm a girl. America thinks Omar is gay. She specifically thinks Omar is gay because he's never asked me to be his girlfriend. Not that she thinks it would be a good idea, since she's convinced I'm too young to have a boyfriend and should concentrate on school.

I hope things never change between Omar and me. America insists that all boys are man-whores and eventually every weasel has to pop. Whatever the heck that means! And why is everybody in my life obsessed with popping? I hope Omar's weasel never pops, and I'm always one of the boys to him.

As I reach the park, I realize that Omar is not alone. There's another boy with him who I don't recognize. Omar is a little shorter than me and way shorter than this guy. Picture a really skinny and awkward Dominican kid with kinky hair, cocoa-colored skin, and green eyes, wearing a *Wolverine* T-shirt, shorts, *Incredible Hulk* socks, helmet, knee pads and elbow pads. Standing next to him is a tall, confident cutie with long blondish hair that falls into his dark brown eyes, holding a Zero Skateboard with a sweet deck covered with skulls, wearing no helmet and no pads, very lean but with nice muscles, shown off by his faded jeans and plain red T-shirt. The guy winks at me and smiles like he's hot stuff. He kind of is. But still. I roll my eyes.

He asks Omar, "Who's this chick again?" Without looking at me, like I'm not standing there in front of him. Omar tells him my name, and the new guy says, "I never met a girl named Destiny before." I reply, "That's right, you haven't!" I say it all tough. I think I channeled my sister for a minute. He winks at me again, and my face gets all hot, and for some reason, I feel like slapping him. I don't know why I get so angry, but there's something about him.

"This is Nicolas," says Omar. "Yasmin's cousin."

"You're Mrs. H's nephew?" I ask. Mrs. H is that R-I-C-H friend of my mom's, Yasmin's mother. I heard something about a relative coming to stay for a while.

"Yeah," he confirms with that killer smile.

"He's from Philadelphia," adds Omar.

"What're you doing in New York?" I ask, and Nicolas starts talking about his family. How his dad's a cabdriver and his mom works in some factory in Philly and his older sister just dropped out of high school. His parents were afraid he'd drop out of high school, too, so they sent him to live with Mr. and Mrs. H. I can tell he really likes that I'm listening to him talk about his family, and I like it, too.

"In other words, his parents couldn't handle him." Omar elbows Nicolas. "They thought that Mr. and Mrs. H and Yasmin would be a good influence. They're sending him to Brandeis for now. Careful. He's a total player."

Nicolas playfully hits Omar on the head with his board.

"*Are* you a player?" I ask Nicolas.

He grins at me all cool. *Player.* I knew it. I roll my eyes again. He almost fooled me with that family stuff.

"We're going to practice jumps," says Omar.

"I can't do jumps," I say. He knows I don't like doing tricks, I just like to ride and ride and ride. That's my thing. Suddenly, Omar gets together with Nicolas and he wants to do jumps?

"You can try," says Omar.

"Sure," agrees Nicolas. "You can try, beautiful."

Beautiful?

"No, I'm going back home. I'm not looking to hurt myself today."

"I'll catch you if you fall, sweetheart." Nicolas softly touches my elbow.

Sweetheart?

"Don't be like that," says Omar and fake punches my shoulder. "What's wrong?"

"Don't be so nosey."

Omar touches his nose like I was making fun of him. He's real self-conscious about his nose. I don't know why. It's not *that* big. He looks at Nicolas all funny and then at me, because Nicolas and I are standing there on Central Park West, staring at each other.

There's just something about Nicolas. I know he's a player. He's winking and flirting, all tall and cute, and he probably flirts with everybody. No thank you. But maybe he's misunderstood. Maybe he's confused because his parents are struggling and sent him away to rich relatives in New York? Maybe he feels a bit lost?

You have to be a more understanding person as you get older. You can't be a little kid anymore. I mean, I'm about to start high school tomorrow. Maybe I should try a jump. Maybe I'll see a different side of Nicolas. Maybe he'll see a different side of me. Maybe he'll be completely bowled over by how smooth and steady I am on my board and give up his player ways because, next to me, no other girl will do.

Ha!

Or I could try to jump and fall and bust my butt and humiliate myself. In front of Nicolas. That would be awful.

I mean, there is something about him. . . .

5 minutes later

JUMP

We push, kick, and coast all the way down Central Park West to Columbus Circle. We roll past the Museum of Natural History on 79th Street, past Strawberry Fields on 72nd (a garden dedicated to John Lennon), until we reach the busy traffic circle at 59th Street. Nicolas is doing some pretty good skateboard tricks. He slides along the edge of the curb using his deck to move forward. Then he grinds along the edge to move forward. Then he ollies by snapping the tail of his board down, sliding his front foot up, and shooting into the air with the board stuck to his feet. He does the tricks, one after the other, like he's preparing for the X Games. Omar and I applaud.

"Wow!"

"Sweet!"

"Nice!"

We head toward the concrete island in the center of the circle, where exhausted pedestrians and tourists hang out on stone benches surrounded by fountains. Nicolas sets up a short ramp using some tough cardboard and a discarded milk crate. I sit on the pedestal of the Christopher Columbus statue and watch. Nicolas flies like a bullet toward the ramp and kicks the board with his front foot to make it flip and spin underneath him. He jumps so far off the ground, I think he's going to decapitate Columbus. He lands at the other end of the short ramp, wheels down, his red T-shirt wet with sweat, and rides back over. We do a high five.

Omar's up next. He takes off toward the ramp, and of course almost kills himself, half-flying, half-falling, board going left, Omar going right, and down he goes, nearly slamming into an old man, who curses at him in thirteen languages. Omar apologizes, gets up, dusts himself off, smiles, and throws his skinny arms in the air to show he's not hurt. A few people clap. Thank God for helmets.

"You're next, Destiny!" shouts Omar.

"No, I'll just watch."

Omar shakes his head and keeps practicing.

Tony Hawk invented eighty tricks, and I can't jump a piece of cardboard? Vanessa Torres, who was my inspiration to start skateboarding and the first girl to win gold at the X Games, would be ashamed of me. But I feel so shy in front of Nicolas. I don't want him to think I'm showing off. I skated slow the whole way here. I know what America would say—you *should* show off in front of guys.

It's nice to have someone who's so good on a board for a change. I mean, Omar's okay, but he doesn't take it seriously. Maybe I could start out with a few small jumps and work my way up. Nicolas would smile at me and then I'd whiz past him and soar into a jump, the highest jump ever attempted—as he gazes up at me in amazement.

I push down on the tail of my board with my foot and feel the tail flex and the board pop up.

Nicolas stops skating and sits down next to me on the pedestal. I can hear Lupe Fiasco playing on his iPod.

"So, um," he says, removing his headphones. "Destiny? Funny name."

"So, um," I answer, leaning back. "Nicolas? Funny face."

I don't believe I said that.

"Funny girl. Speak Spanish?"

"*Sí.*"

"My cousin goes to your school."

I nod. "Columbus Prep is a private school, but my sister and I are on serious scholarships. We're not rich or anything."

Why do I feel like I need to explain?

He stares at me like I'm one of those penguins in the Central Park Zoo, flapping around on the rocks.

"Omar told me you're gonna have a *quinceañera.* My sister had one a couple of years ago in Philly."

"How was it?"

"Fun," says Nicolas. "I danced like crazy. I'm a good dancer."

"Modest, too," I note and spin the wheels on my board.

"Yeah."

And we smile at each other. Is it my imagination or is Nicolas Hernandez checking me out like I'm more than a new friend?

"When you have your *quinceañera*," he says, "can I come?"

"Uh . . . yeah."

"I'm a good dancer," he promises.

"I've heard that about you."

"From who?"

"From you about a minute ago."

"Oh, yeah." He laughs and spins a wheel on my board. "Right."

"I'm getting a Plan B for my birthday," I tell him.

"Nice," he says. "Do you like graphic novels?"

"Sure." I've never actually read one.

He pulls one out of his backpack and hands it to me. It's Neil Gaiman's *Sandman*.

"Have you read it?"

I shake my head and play with my ponytail. "What's it about?"

"Dreams and stuff mixed in with fantasy, very cool."

"I love dreams!" I say and then realize how stupid that sounds. "I mean, mine are pretty wack sometimes." I flip through some of the pages.

"You'd probably like this, then. You can borrow it when I'm done."

"Thanks." We sit there smiling again.

Is it my imagination or is he *seriously* flirting now?

I wonder which is more the real Nicolas, you know? Like the way he's looking at me right now, all sensitive, or the cool skater guy. I guess it would be nice if he were attracted to me, just a little bit. But I would never let him kiss me, if he tried. I mean, he is a player, right? America would kill me. Push come to shove, I need my *cara*, my arms, my long spider legs, and my life. Thank you, Nicolas. I know I'm hard to resist. But no, our love was never meant to be. Don't speak. Don't speak.

We're going on like that, smiling at each other like two dopes, when Omar comes over.

"We could go to Riverside Park," Omar suggests and looks at Nicolas, who shrugs.

The Riverside Skateboarding Park is all the way west near the Hudson River. The park has five ramps, half pipes, quarter pipes, and rails where you can practice tricks. You have to have a helmet and kneepads and elbow pads and a guardian's permission to get in there. Nicolas doesn't have any of those things, and I don't like doing tricks. It doesn't make sense.

"You're not having fun here?" I ask Omar, feeling sorry that we've been ignoring him. I really didn't mean to.

"It's okay. Not as much fun as we usually have, though." Omar glances at Nicolas and blurts out, "Destiny's really good on her board."

"You mean, I'm really good for a girl," I say, all snotty.

"Nah. You're good. Period. I don't know why you're just sitting down."

"I'm resting," I say and glare at him for being both very nice and very annoying.

"Maybe you two would rather go boarding together." Omar's looking at me and Nicolas pretty intensely. I guess we really have been ignoring him.

"No," I insist. "I can plan my own day, but thank you."

"DESTINY!" Someone shrieks my name like I'm lost on the moon and they've been searching for me all day by space shuttle.

"Mami?"

"Surprise!" my mother cries, triumphantly from behind the wheel of our Pontiac. I know Nicolas isn't R-I-C-H, but I'm embarrassed that he sees our old rusty car in the crosswalk. I close my eyes and try to make it disappear. My mother is supposed to be at work. I tell myself this is just one of my vivid stress dreams. I take a deep breath and open my eyes. This nightmare is real. The Pontiac is still rusty and still there in the crosswalk. I think I even hear it laughing at me.

This is NOT my day.

1 minute later

PONTIAC

"Hey!" yells Stephanie, jumping out of the backseat of the car and grinning at me when she spies Nicolas. Stephanie is larger than life. She's five-nine with long braided hair, and she's all *Top Model*. She's wearing large, dark Jackie O sunglasses, a black-and-white halter-top, skinny jeans, and gladiator sandals. You wouldn't believe how many guys at school were in love with Stephanie last year. I'm not kidding, it must have been at least forty or fifty. And she doesn't have to do anything special to get them to fall in love with her. She's beautiful without showing it off. Sometimes it's a little depressing being Stephanie's friend.

If that isn't enough, she has a boyfriend named Jesse who loves her like crazy. And she's actually done a bit of modeling. I went with her on a shoot for an Old Navy newspaper ad. Glamour isn't really my thing, but it made my life seem boring in comparison. She's using the modeling money to help pay for college, not that she has to. Her parents are loaded. But Stephanie is beautiful *and* considerate. That's why we're friends. (And it's nice to hang out with someone taller than me.)

"Dude!" That's Erin, shaking her head at me from the

backseat. Her short, brown, curly hair and gray eyes are almost hidden under a Sundance baseball cap, and she's wearing a Liberty basketball jersey. In case you can't tell, she has two obsessions—basketball and movies. Erin was MVP last year on the JV girl's basketball team.

Erin thinks she's hilarious—and Stephanie and I usually agree—but she goes too far sometimes.

"What's up, Virgin Mary?" Erin asks me.

See? I made the mistake of telling Erin that the *quince*, in certain religious circles, is also about a girl "dedicating herself to the Virgin Mary." (America *loves* that.)

Stephanie giggles from the curb. They think showing up here with my mother is funny. Stephanie's black and Erin's Jewish, so they both know what it is to be different, but neither of them really gets what it's like to live in two worlds, to have parents who were born in another country and who push you to succeed here but at the same time, keep pulling you back.

"Dude!" Erin yells again, patting the empty seat next to her. "C'mon!"

I absolutely *hate* when Erin calls me dude in front of cute guys who may or may not be flirting shamelessly with me.

I glance at Nicolas, who is still sitting next to me. No reaction. Is that good or bad?

"We're getting *flan*!" yells my mother, leaning her blonde head out of the car window. "And going over some details for your *quince*."

"Why aren't you at work?" I ask, jumping down off the pedestal.

"I'm going in later."

Some cars start honking for my mom to move.

"Get in the car, *nena!*"

Omar has already hopped in the backseat with Erin, skateboard and all, smacking his lips and mouthing the word *flan*. It's amazing how a slice of sweet custard can change Omar's mood.

"You, uh, want to come with us, Nicolas?" I ask.

I have to be polite. I *have* to ask Nicolas if he wants to come, too. Politeness, that's all it is.

"Nah," says Nicolas. "I gotta split. But give me your number so I can text you. Maybe it'll be your *destiny* to see me again."

I quickly give him my number. He plugs it into his cell and winks at me. Okay, he is the best winker! He skates off into the crosswalk, past the Pontiac, toward Central Park.

The truth? My entire dating experience has consisted of a ten-minute kissing session with David Silva behind the curtain at the sixth grade graduation dance . . . after which, the only thing I could think to say was "Do you like Ping-Pong?" I mean, there was a boy who was "in love" with me (he said) at the start of last year, Kevin. He was eight inches shorter than me (at least it wasn't a foot), and it didn't really bother me, although Stephanie thought that was just plain *wrong*. And Erin said that it looked like I was babysitting him. But he was really easy to talk to and joke around with, and we spent tons of time together in the computer lab. When we went to see *Mamma Mia* on Broadway with our class, we held hands during the show. But nothing ever happened (and

I mean nothing!). I wasn't attracted to him, not like he was to me. After a while, it got a little weird, and we kept coming up with excuses not to hang out. I think, in a way, I wanted a boyfriend mostly because I'd never had one before. But I've never had mumps, either. Still, I wonder sometimes, what if I had a boyfriend that I liked as much as he liked me?

Nicolas has my number. He's going to text me. What does that mean? Does that mean he really wants to see me again? Everybody trades cell numbers. No, he'll never text or call. But if he weren't so full of himself . . . I'd think maybe he's kind of clever. And he's got that blondish hair that falls into his eyes, which is kind of a shame because they're nice eyes. Very dark and mysterious. . . .

"See ya!" I call out and wave, real cute, like I imagine Stephanie would do. No need to look like a spazz. Except Nicolas misses it because he's skating away. Nice one, Destiny.

"Destiny and blond boy sitting in a tree!" I hear Erin chanting.

I spin around to face my mother and my friends. Stephanie gets into the passenger seat. I squeeze into the back and stare out the window into the park. Did Nicolas just turn around and wave at me? At *me*? Or at Omar? Nah, not Omar. Nicolas is totally crushing on me. Ha!

"K-I-S-S—"

"Erin!" I snap. Stephanie and my mother laugh.

I feel a poke in my ribs. Omar beams at me. "*Flan* good."

I'm squashed up against him as the car pulls away.

"Who was that boy?" my mother asks.

"Nicolas Hernandez," says Omar. "Mrs. H's nephew."

"Ah!" my mom gushes. "So that's the famous Nicolas!"

I look in the rearview mirror, and there's my mother grinning at me like a meerkat on Animal Planet about to bite down on a bug.

I stare out the window again, hoping for a last glimpse of Nicolas as he disappears farther and farther into the green trees, sunshine, the freedom of Central Park.

20 minutes later

LA CARIDAD

We're at La Caridad restaurant on 78th and Broadway. I can sort of understand why Stephanie gets a kick out of the whole *quince* thing and came running when my mother called her. She's already picked out a fabulous purple dress for all the *damas* to wear. But Erin? My sister in all things Tomboy? I'm wondering what else my mother bribed her with besides *flan*. IMAX movie tickets? And then there's my skate buddy in crime, Omar, waiting to stuff his belly. *Et tu*, Omar?

"*Ay.*" My mother sighs, shaking her head. She's dressed for work in a red blouse, a gray skirt, and low red heels. "We have less than two months and so much to do! We still have to stuff and send the invitations. I want you to address them by hand, Destiny. No excuses." She turns to my friends. "Would you believe she has not chosen a *caballero* yet?"

"Well," says Stephanie, who's still wearing her sunglasses inside, "she can be pretty hardheaded when she wants to be."

Erin nods and pushes back her Sundance cap. "The girl's got chutzpah. She just hides it sometimes."

"I thought we agreed that I don't need a *caballero*?" say.

"Maybe you all," my mom stares at Omar, "can help Destiny change her mind?"

The waiter brings over our *flan*. Omar's expression of gratitude is unmistakable. He attacks the custard like it's his last meal.

"What if Destiny skips this *Q* thing and takes her closest friends to a Knicks game instead?" suggests Erin.

"Ha-ha," I say. For some reason, Stephanie and Erin never use the word *quinceañera*, let alone *quince*.

"Destiny needs an escort, a *caballero*," repeats my mother, handing a pink folder to Omar (like that's not a big hint) with a white cloud on the front. I've seen it a million times already. Inside the cloud, she's written "Destiny's *quinceañera*" with a red Sharpie in her best flowery script. Both the i's are dotted with smiley faces, and inside the folder are pictures of stuff like tiaras, rings, earrings, crosses, Bibles, rosaries, scepters, floral bouquets, guest books, photo albums, invitations, reception cards, ceremony pillows, limos, and even a throne.

"So what does the *cuba-lero* do?" asks Stephanie, delicately slicing a fork through her *flan*. "What exactly happens at this thing?"

I nod at Omar, who has been to five *quinces* already and is always dying to show off his knowledge of stuff that nobody else really cares about. I guess I also want to make it up to him for ignoring him in Columbus Circle earlier. I point n pressing PLAY.

ipes melted sugar off his chin and clears his throat: ceañera has two sections, a mass and a party. During the mass, fourteen candles are lit, and the mother places a tiara on her daughter's head, and the father changes her flat shoes into high heels, and the *quinceañera*—or birthday girl—gives her parents a childhood doll symbolizing that she's become a young woman. Then the 'young woman' is escorted into the second section of the *quince*, her birthday party, by a boy called a *caballero*, which is Spanish for like a knight in shining armor. The *quinceañera* and the *caballero* go into the party behind her court, which includes seven girls called *damas* and seven guys called *chambelanes*. The *quinceañera* has to do this waltz with her father. Then the court dances. Then the guests dance. Then all the men and boys take turns dancing with the *quinceañera*. Then there's a toast, and cake is served."

Omar pauses to rub his belly. "The whole thing looks like a wedding. But it's really about when a girl becomes a woman."

I say, "Yeah, just like that. Poof!"

Omar laughs. "Did you know the *quinceañera* goes all the way back to the Aztec Indians, in, like, the fifteen hundreds?"

"Wow!" Erin laughs with him. "Destiny is older than I thought!"

"So is the *cuba-lero* supposed to be her boyfriend or what?" asks Stephanie, getting to the heart of the matter as always.

"Uh, not necessarily," I say. "He's just her escort, her

date, the guy on her arm."

"Ah, her arm candy!" says Stephanie.

"Her stud." Erin points her fork at Omar.

"The *caballero* has to wear a tuxedo and take dance lessons," Omar goes on, "because he's supposed to do a special waltz with the *Q*-girl after she dances with her dad."

My mother stares at Omar. "I didn't realize you knew so much about *quinceañeras*!" She eats her *flan* and examines Omar as if she's never really seen him before. I can practically see the word *CABALLERO* in a thought bubble above her head.

Omar fidgets in his seat. "I know a lot of stuff." His eyes lock on the pink folder in his hands, like he is afraid to look up. OMG! I think Omar wants to be my *caballero*! That would be so weird. Wouldn't it?

Then my mom whips out a magazine she's been carrying around in her handbag since August.

Are you ready? The magazine is called *Quince Beat: Your Q Planner in English y Español*. The first twenty pages show girls modeling dresses straight out of *Gone with the Wind* in front of cheesy backdrops of winding staircases. The magazine is full of party guides, hair and makeup tips, everything you "need to know."

My mother flips through some more pages and flashes this huge ad of a skinny, perfect-looking girl wearing a hideous, hot-pink dress. The caption reads "Color is *caliente!*" Then she shows us this article about a poor girl from the Bronx whose family couldn't afford a *quinceañera,* so Disney World gave her one. They have pics of her dancing with

Prince Charming and blowing out candles on a cake shaped like a castle. My mother goes into a saga about how when she was a girl, they were very-very-very poor like that girl in *Quince Beat* and how sad her *quinceañera* was compared to the ones the other girls had, how they laughed at her the next week for wearing her aunt's old prom dress and serving potato chips on paper plates.

Poor Mami. I get a lump in my throat. I can't help it. I've heard this story before, but it gets me every time, and in spite of all her *telenovela* drama, I know it's all true. It's part of the reason why I said yes to having a *quinceañera* in the first place.

I must've gotten very quiet, because my mother asks me, "What's wrong?" I respond with my usual, "Nothing," but I'm thinking about the rent being late and that my parents can't afford all of this Sweet Fifteen stuff—no matter how much my mom wants it. And that Erin and Stephanie wouldn't understand all this if I told them. Omar would. Maybe Nicolas?

Confession: I'm a little bit ashamed about my family's lack of money and what my parents do. Maybe it's because I began going to private school when I was twelve, and Stephanie's father is the CEO of some company and her mother is a magazine editor, and Erin's father is a scientist and her mother is a professor.

And did I mention that my mom is a receptionist at a doctor's office and my dad is a doorman at a fancy apartment building?

"Well," Stephanie says to my mom, "I think it's amazing how you grew up so poor and now you can afford to throw this giant party and—"

"I promised America that I would have only *chambelanes* and *damas*," I cut in. "No *caballero*."

Erin touches my arm. "Are you really okay?"

"What?"

"You should see your face," says Stephanie.

"I'm just here for the *flan*," I tell them.

That's when I hear a loud sigh. The kind that only mothers can make. I glance over, and mine has her hand on her forehead.

"What's up, Mrs. Lozada?" Erin asks.

My mom does the trying-to-manage-a-smile-but-can't thing and closes her eyes. She groans, clutches my hand, and declares, "If only Destiny would decide to have a *caballero,* it would make me so happy, ease the stress of all this work I'm doing."

I look from Stephanie to Erin to Omar. "You guys think it's a good idea for me to have a *caballero*?"

Erin shrugs.

"Definitely!" says Stephanie.

Omar shovels more *flan*. "Well, at all the *quinces* I went to, the girl had a *caballero*. He doesn't have to be her boyfriend or anything."

I think about Nicolas and how he could maybe be my escort.

First problem, I'm really self-conscious about dancing.

When I dance, sirens go off and police show up with searchlights, calling for backup. Step away from the dance floor, Ms. Lozada!

Then I start worrying about how Omar would feel if Nicolas were my escort, but I shouldn't since we're all just friends. Right?

And then there's the rent. Maybe I could pitch in and help pay for some stuff? I can talk to my father and ask him to let me babysit or something?

I think and worry and think and worry, until I finally say, "Okay, Mami. I'll choose a *caballero* by the end of next week."

"*Perfecto*." My mother sits up in her seat, healthy as a burro, acting like she's about to dance a *salsa*, a *merengue*, ballet, and some modern jazz steps. It's a miracle! A blessed miracle!

She orders another round of *flan* and declares that I am on my way to "becoming a woman." I'm not sure I like the sound of that. Stephanie starts calling me *la* woman, which she thinks is so cute, and I'm picturing her walking down a runway with my foot in her ass. Erin's nodding and nodding, trying not to laugh, and eating her *flan*. Omar stares at me all funny.

My mother kisses me on both cheeks. Stephanie hugs me and tells me it will be fabulous, and she's got some ideas for boys from school (oh, lord, that starts tomorrow!) who could be my *caballero*. I don't know how I'll have the heart to tell my sister.

My mom holds up *Quince Beat* and points to a tuxedo. "Your *caballero* will be so handsome in this!"

Don't push it, Mami, I want to say, but her face is all lit up.

"I told America you'd see it my way," she says.

I give her my best "you're killing me" expression. "You didn't tell America we were coming here to talk about the *caballero*?" I ask.

"I did," answers my mother. "It's your *quince*. She understands."

Here we go again!

10 minutes later

THE JEZEBELS

Once we leave La Caridad, everyone jumps back into the Pontiac. Except me. All I can think about is that America knew my mother would convince me to have a *caballero*. Something's coming. I just don't know when.

"I'm going to ride home on my board," I say.

"I'll go with you," says Omar.

"Alone," I add.

He shrugs and stays in the backseat.

My mom waves and blows me kisses. Stephanie assures me again that we'll make this work. Erin makes a fist and says, "Keep the faith." And Omar pouts as the car drives off.

I hop on my board and kick off into the street. I roll along toward Central Park West, then turn left and go north, wondering if I'll bump into Nicolas somehow, wondering if I should head back over to Columbus Circle, if he'd be there, waiting for me. But why would he?

I'm totally daydreaming as I glide toward 97th Street. The sound of someone whistling snaps me out of it. I look up and see my sister's friend Maritza on the corner by the park.

Maritza is very pretty and petite. She's built like a mini-JLo but with short, shockingly pink hair and cat-glasses. At the moment, she's wearing black jeans, a sky blue T-shirt, and combat boots. Maritza wants to be a writer some day, and she gave America a copy of *The House on Mango Street* by Sandra Cisneros, which I've read three times. She's giggling and headed straight toward me.

"What's up, Maritza?" I ask carefully as I jump off my board and pick it up.

I hear more whistling and the familiar clinking and clanging of many silver bracelets. Maritza's eyes dart behind me.

I turn my head, and there's my sister's friend Hailey. Hailey is an Amazon with long blonde hair. She plans on being either a veterinarian or a doctor, plus she's six feet tall, so she can be kind of intimidating. Today, her blue eyes have this sinister gleam, and I realize she's wearing the same outfit as Maritza.

She's headed straight for me, too, and they're both giggling now. Oh, yes, my sister and her friends are all freaks. They call themselves The Jezebels.

The Jezebels are a private feminist club of three that has been meeting since seventh grade. America is the club president. They keep an "office" at Tom's Restaurant on Broadway and I'm not sure what they do there, but they always come back fired up about stuff. They all plan on going to the same college: Sarah Lawrence.

The real Jezebel was this queen from the Bible who was considered a slut. But America says Jezebel was a strong woman who got persecuted by men who didn't like how she wore her makeup or what she chose to believe or who she loved and decided to turn her into dog food. (My mother

HATES that they call themselves The Jezebels and has suggested that they call themselves The Sunflowers instead.)

They have Jezebel Nights—sleepovers—one Friday of every month, when they eat takeout from Tom's Restaurant and discuss the battle of the sexes and play Ms. Pac Man on the computer all night long.

Last year, The Jezebels were dating three guys that have a band called *Los Guapos*. They were a happy family of six and did everything together until Tomas and America broke up. Things have been a little tense ever since. Tomas still calls all the time, but America hangs up on him. Ah, love.

"What're you guys up to?" I ask, trying to sound casual. No answer. I don't know what the game is, but I'll play along for now. America's friends hardly ever give me the time of day, and I'm secretly a little bit flattered. I giggle, too, and pretend to make a run for it. Before I reach the curb, Maritza blocks my way while Hailey comes up behind me and lifts me off the ground. Maritza grabs my skateboard. People on the street ignore us, which is typical for New York.

A green Beetle comes screeching around the corner, and I recognize it immediately as Hailey's car. The door opens. I'm carried in by Hailey, and we're all giggling now.

My sister is smiling at me from the driver's seat. Her wild black hair looks wilder than usual, and she's wearing the same combo of jeans, T-shirt, and boots as Maritza and Hailey. I see that on the back of the shirts, they've written in thick black marker, The Jezebel Girls Club of America.

America asks me, "Are you a stupid girl?"

"No!"

"I've heard rumors that say otherwise."

We drive.

"What are you talking about?" I ask.

"Disinfectant phase one." America is in command mode now. Maritza and Hailey pull out perfume bottles.

"Hello and welcome to Macy's!" says Hailey, smiling like a robot.

"Try our new scent, Not-So-Sweet-Fifteen!" Maritza adds.

"Cover your eyes!" orders America, still driving.

I quickly do it.

They spray me all over. It smells like vanilla.

"What is that for?" I ask, coughing.

"The stink of the *caballero* is still on you," explains America. "We don't want to risk any possible contamination. I called Mami, and she told me that you folded like a Jennifer Convertible. I'm not mad at you. I've had my shots. I'm immune to *caballeros*, but Mami's pressure could make anybody crack. We're here to save the day."

Hailey examines my eyes, ears, and teeth. "How's your cholesterol?"

"I'm fourteen."

"Let me check your heart."

"No."

"You could have a heart murmur you don't know about." Hailey pulls an old stethoscope out of her bag and listens to my heart. "She's good. No physical disabilities affecting her thinking."

Maritza goes into her purse and hands me a paperback

book, *1984* by George Orwell. "It's about brainwashing," she says.

"I love you madly." America is watching me in the rearview mirror. "You know that, right, Dusty?"

"Yes, Merry," I say. I peer out of the window. We're back on Broadway and heading farther uptown.

"What does it mean to be a stupid girl, Dusty?" America answers for me: "If you keep doing the *quince* Mami's way, with tiaras and *caballeros* and a stone-age ceremony that makes you give up parts of yourself, that's what you'll be. Just another stupid girl. Do you get what I'm saying?"

"I guess so," I say. "But isn't it too late to stop Mami?"

"NOT having a *caballero* is your way to show the world what a unique individual you are."

"Amen!" adds Maritza.

A unique individual? Is that really me? I want it to be me. I thought it was me. But what if it's not?

"You can't go through life," America continues, "like a scrap of paper carried by the wind, with no destination, other than what fate or Mami has in store. I was too soft when I let her manipulate you into having this *quince*. Refusing to have a *caballero* is just the tip of the iceberg."

"It's too late," I say again.

"No!" shouts America, stopping at a light. "You will take back the night! You will take back your birthday! You will take back the *quinceañera*!"

Hailey and Maritza applaud.

"But what does that mean exactly?" I ask.

Hailey digs into her bag and pulls out a thick manila folder and a laptop.

"It's obvious that we need to make a stronger case against the *caballero*," says my sister. "You shouldn't experience certain things too young. Take my word for it."

I know she's talking about Tomas. I know she's trying to protect me, and I don't want to get hurt, either. I get enough bruises from my skateboard every time I fall. But then I think about Nicolas. . . .

"You're starting ninth grade tomorrow," America points out. "I didn't have a boyfriend until I got to eleventh. You're too young to get wrapped up in this whole *caballero*-escort-date-boy thing."

"Uh-huh."

"You're my little Dusty. I don't want you getting hurt by some stupid boy now. There is going to be plenty of time for that later."

"A *caballero* is not a boyfriend," I say.

"Right." America smirks at Maritza and Hailey as she begins to parallel park on Broadway. They smirk back.

"What're we doing?" I glance out the window and realize that I've been driven to Tom's Restaurant (which is not only the official Jezebel office but also where they filmed the outside of the *Seinfeld* diner).

"We're going to have a fair trial of the *caballero*," America declares.

"Once," says Maritza.

"And for all," Hailey finishes.

"And Destiny?" America turns off the car, then leans

back in the driver's seat and faces me.

"Uh-huh?"

"No pressure," she whispers.

The three of them cackle.

"Right," I say.

No pressure at all.

POWERPOINT

The Jezebels brief me over Diet Cokes and fries. They want to put my future, unknown *caballero* on trial, complete with research, handouts, and a PowerPoint presentation on *The History of Women's Rights.* I don't know how they pulled it together so fast. It's like they were just waiting for the opportunity.

After Tom's, we go back to our apartment. My mother is on the red sofa in the living room. I'm sitting between her and America. Maritza is standing near the turntable where my parents play their old *salsa* records. Natasha starts rubbing against Hailey's ankles and purring loudly. Hailey scoops Natasha up in her arms and kisses her on the mouth. Maritza makes a disgusted face.

America sets up the laptop on the coffee table, and the PowerPoint begins. It's *really* long. I force myself to pay attention while my mother drinks a mug of *El Pico* coffee (Latino Therapy) to calm herself down. My father, wearing his black doorman jacket, sits deep in thought in his rocker in front of the TV, which unfortunately, is not on.

When the PowerPoint is over, Hailey closes the laptop, Maritza crosses her arms, and America jumps up and stares at my mother. "Can you hear me now?"

I'm imagining the *Daily News* headline: 18-YEAR-OLD LATINA KILLED AFTER HER MOM DECIDES ENOUGH IS ENOUGH. Ambulance driver reports: "It was awful. The poor girl was knocked clean out of her bra, and we still can't find the head."

Everyone looks at my dad, and we all realize that he's not deep in thought but fully asleep, and snoring softly. He's just come home from work and still has to cook dinner.

"Papi!" shouts America.

"Jon!"

My father wakes up and mumbles, "Burning witches is wrong."

Maritza shakes her head. Hailey snickers.

"We're way past that part, Papi," I tell him.

"Oh. What part are we on?"

"We're fighting a system that objectifies women," says America. "We have to extricate our bodies from this." She holds up my mother's *Quince Beat* magazine.

"Okay." My father gazes at me. "Are we still talking about your *quince*?"

I shrug. "I think so."

My mother snatches the magazine out of America's hand as if it's her third child. "What's wrong with this?"

"All those girls are stereotypically beautiful," says Hailey, who *is* stereotypically beautiful.

"That's what people like looking at," my mother insists. "Would you be happier if they were stereotypically ugly?"

"We'd be happy if they looked normal," says Maritza and runs her hand through her pink hair.

48

"What does any of this have to do with Destiny's *caballero*?" asks my mother.

"We're tired of being victims of Avon!" says America.

"Don't you dare," my mother whispers.

My father closes his eyes again.

Fact check: My mom has been selling Avon cosmetics for extra spending money ever since I can remember. In our house, there are two things you don't criticize: the baby Jesus and Avon. I don't think I've ever seen my mother without her makeup on.

America takes a deep, exhausted breath. "Don't you get it?"

"*Yo no comprendo*," answers my mother.

Maritza whips a copy of *A Room of One's Own* by Virginia Woolf from her bag and hands it to my mom.

"We have to change the status quo," says Hailey, "if we're going to have more and more female doctors."

"And writers," adds Maritza.

"And lawyers," adds America.

"You girls can go change the status quo at your prom," says my mother. "Please leave Destiny's *caballero* alone."

"Weren't you paying attention to the presentation?" America points at Hailey's laptop. "Today's career women still don't make an equal dollar for every dollar that men make doing the same job."

"But what does that have to do with *caballeros*?" My mother sighs, stroking Natasha, who has jumped onto her lap and is purring like an airplane engine.

"Look at Mrs. Salazar," says America.

"What about her?"

"Remember when we went to their house last Easter and not one of those men lifted a finger? They sat there and ate and burped like kings while Mrs. Salazar and Sofia ran around like Energizer bunnies! What about what they did to poor Sofia!"

"Poor Sofia," Maritza agrees.

"Poor, poor Sofia," echoes Hailey.

My mother looks at America and then my father, and asks, "Can we sell her?"

He opens his eyes. "I'm afraid not."

"Can we move?"

"What do you think, Destiny?" my father asks me.

"They'll only find us again."

My sister and The Jezebels glare at me like I'm conspiring with the enemy. But America is right about the Salazars. It's like being stuck in one of those old sitcoms where the mother wears an apron and talks about kitchen appliances while the father smokes his pipe. Sofia, the Salazars' daughter, was expected to be a good girl, to be quiet and smile and wear plain dresses and flats and give up her childhood fun when she hit fifteen. I had always liked her because outside her house, she was smart and tough and wasn't afraid to dream anything. She wanted to go to college. She wanted to see the world. Instead, she married her boyfriend after high school, and they had a baby and that was that.

"Maybe we should be more like the Salazars," America continues. "Papi can stop doing his share of the housework and sit around and watch us wait on him while Mami cooks and the food poisoning bills pile up." Without waiting for a response, she adds, "I'll need you both to sign these."

And with that, The Jezebels give us their last handout.

Destiny's List of Demands for Her Quinceañera

#1. Destiny will Not give up her sneakers for heels.
#2. Destiny will Not give up her favorite childhood doll.
#3. Destiny will Not wear a dress.
#4. Destiny will Not be escorted by a boy.

Approved by her loving parents:

_____

Jon and Miriam Lozada

"Are you out of your mind?" My mother peers up from the list. "No dress? I already ordered it. It'll be here soon."

"You can return the dress and get your deposit back," says America.

"Why have the *quince* at all?" my mother declares. "Why not just get a table at some greasy spoon, order chicken nuggets, and call it a night?"

America nods. "I like it!"

My mother glares at my father. "Jon?"

My father raises his eyes to the ceiling and shakes his head as if praying for guidance.

I just sit there. I don't even know where to begin; this whole thing has spun so far out of my reach. And no one is looking to me for anything.

"Would you put the Statue of Liberty on a skateboard?" asks America. "No, of course not. So why would you put Destiny Lozada in a dress? Some things simply don't go together."

"She looks beautiful in a dress." My mother touches my knee.

It's true. I do. Ha!

"That's not the point, Mother!"

America's not really a dress Nazi. She wears dresses when she wants, and sometimes gets very girly-girl with makeup and heels when she goes out on a date or to a party or something. Me? Yeah, I'm not so comfortable wearing dresses, but I'm not totally against them. I guess I'm more of a sneakers and baggy jeans kind of chick. Not exactly tomboy. Not exactly girly-girl. Somewhere in the middle.

But maybe wearing a dress for the *quince* wouldn't be so bad. It's a one-time thing, right? Could be cool?

America takes a piece of notebook paper from her pocket and unfolds it. "I've gone through Mami's pink folder and done the math on this *quince* and how much you guys are paying so far in terms of deposits."

My father starts rocking in his chair as America goes on. "You've already spent almost two thousand dollars, that I know of, on deposits for the church, reception hall, caterer, photographer, dress, and invites. Then there's still the DJ, flowers, decorations, *and* a town car for a grand total, when you make full payments, of about ten thousand dollars, probably more."

I knew my *quince* was expensive, but I had no idea it was THAT expensive. TEN THOUSAND DOLLARS!

America scans the room in disbelief. "Mami also wanted a live band. I'm trying to save you guys money!"

My mother sighs her huge sigh. My father keeps rocking, eyes closed.

What are they thinking! We can't possibly afford this. The rent is already late? I wonder if my father is thinking the same thing.

"America." My mom stands up. "We appreciate that you're trying to save us money, but no escort? No *caballero*? What does that have to do with saving money?"

"Boys will use you and abuse you and leave you for dead." America stuffs the notebook paper back in her pocket.

I can't help breaking in. "Wait, aren't there any good boys out there?"

"She's talking about the good ones." My father laughs with his eyes still closed.

"Yeah," says America, glancing at Maritza and Hailey. "The bad ones are worse."

"Aha!" my mother cries. "So that's what this is really about? Tomas!"

America looks as if she's been harpooned in the heart.

"Well," says Hailey, "Tomas isn't really bad, he's just—"

Maritza chimes in, "He made a—"

"This meeting is adjourned!" America cuts them off. "Once you sign the demands, Mami, you'll get no more trouble from me."

"If I sign this," says my mother, smiling slyly, "will you all come to the *quince*?"

"Yeah!" says Hailey. "Sure."

"Yay!" Maritza claps. "Everybody wins!"

America scowls at them for breaking ranks. "Never!"

My mother shakes her head. "Why are you so frustrating?"

America laughs. "You want a mirror?"

My mother blows air kisses at her. "*Te quiero mucho*."

"I love you, too. C'mon, Dusty. C'mon, Jezebels."

"Will you two soldiers be staying for dinner?" my mother calls out to Hailey and Maritza as they follow America to our bedroom.

"*Sí*," answers Maritza.

"I just have to call my parents," says Hailey.

"Table for six," my father notes and heads to the kitchen.

My mother is left holding America's demands—clicking her tongue and shaking her head—as I follow The Jezebels and America into our room. But this fight isn't over yet. I know my mother, and I know my sister. Forced to choose, I wouldn't take on either one of them in the ring.

After our *paella* dinner, where any talk about the *quince* was prohibited, I go back to my room, change into my PJs, slide into bed, and try to read a chapter of *1984*. I can hardly believe I'm starting high school tomorrow. Today was such an insane day, I didn't get a chance to worry about it. And now my brain is too tired to try.

Soon my eyes close.

Suddenly America comes in and shouts, "Let's go wait in

line for tickets to see Shakespeare in the Park!"

"We already saw it," I say. "And we have school tomorrow. And isn't that only in the summer?"

"C'mon, it's a special show. Mami and Papi gave the okay."

Is this night never going to end?

It's almost midnight. I'm hot and sweaty, and we're sitting with The Jezebels on white blankets on a patch of rocky dirt near the Delacorte Theater in Central Park. They don't hand out tickets until the morning for tomorrow night's show, but people are already camped out when we get there. We eat M&Ms and wash them down with ginger ale. America practices her Japanese with Maritza, going over possessive verbs, and I'm telling Hailey about my favorite constellations and pointing out as many of them as I can find.

I must have fallen asleep at some point, because the next thing I know, it's morning, and I'm worried that I'm going to miss my first day of school, and the line starts moving and America yells, "*¡Vámonos!*" We're about to get our tickets when my mother shows up and informs us that she wants to go to the South Street Seaport.

"We've been waiting here all night!" America argues. "We have no interest in seeing tourists on parade. The only place we're going is to this play."

"You're coming with me." My mother grabs my right arm.

"No, she's not." My sister grabs my left arm.

They both pull at me, yelling, "Yes! No! Yes! No! Destiny!"

I finally break loose. I'm running, running, running until I get to a field full of sparkly pink and emerald green flowers. I lose a sneaker, but I keep on running. I lose my other sneaker, but I don't stop. Then I see that my feet are transforming into roots. Soon I can't run anymore and I'm sticking to the ground and leaves are coming out of my mouth, my ears, my nose. I can't speak. I can't hear. I can't breathe. My feet and arms and legs are growing into gigantic, thick branches as my mother and America appear out of nowhere . . .

HOLDING AXES!

"We're going to help you," they say, and they chop and chop and chop and chop at me until . . .

"Ahhhhhh . . . !"

I FALL. . . .

That's when I open my eyes and sit up and find that I'm actually still in bed, *1984* open on my lap. I look around the room. America's at the computer, and my mother's standing at the door in her nightgown and slippers.

"What happened?" Mami asks.

"Nothing," I say, squinting. "I'm fine."

"You fell asleep reading your book," America says. "And then you screamed. Another one of your freaky nightmares?"

"Yeah."

My mother blows me a kiss and whispers, "Tomorrow we stuff the *quince* envelopes."

"We'll discuss," says my sister. Mami closes the door. America goes back to the computer.

I try to go back to *1984*, but I can't.

I'm about to turn fifteen for the first and last time in my life. Not to mention that I'm about to start high school.

Trouble, anyone? This is only the beginning. I wish this year was over already.

I'm just lying in bed, paralyzed, when I get a text from a number I don't recognize:

You are the most beautiful girl I've ever seen! Skate15

ACT TWO

the next morning

YASMIN

All night I had dreams about Nicolas and his Skate15 text. Nicolas! It has to be Nicolas! And if he were a player, why would he go through the trouble of sending me a text and being all mysterious? He's really just misunderstood. That's what I think. He really does like me. I'm his new sweetheart, and he's my Skate15. Ha! Maybe he wants to be my *caballero*? If that's true, what would I do about America and her demands? I should have texted him back last night, but I totally froze because he called me "beautiful." I mean, what do you say to that? I'll think of something.

But I don't have time to dwell on it this morning. I have to get to school. It's official. I'm in high school. HIGH SCHOOL.

I head to the kitchen for breakfast, but I stop outside the doorway and listen. It's obvious my parents are having a fight.

"It's not personal, Jon. They're not saying you're a bad person; they're saying that you don't have enough savings or collateral for the loan—"

"They're saying that I'm not *hombre* enough to take care of my own family!"

Aw, man! I know that my *quinceañera* is the reason my father needs to take out a loan, and however crappy I felt before, now I feel ten times worse.

"Look, these things are a formula," my mother explains. "Banks examine the cold, hard numbers. Jon, you're a good father. You *do* take care of your family. Nobody blames—"

"But I should be able to—"

"Nothing to be sorry about, *amor*. You gave it a shot. We'll figure something out. We always do. Remember, I'd rather be poor with you than rich without you."

My dad says he'll ask to work double shifts. My parents have always worked their schedules so we have breakfast and dinner all together. I can't imagine my dad not being there. It makes my heart hurt.

"No," my mom tells him. "You can't work day and night."

"I used to do it when you were pregnant."

"That's true and we thank you, but your old bones are not what they used to be."

My father doesn't laugh. He keeps pushing the double shifts, and my mom keeps saying no until they're almost screaming, something they never do as a rule (since they both grew up with parents who screamed a lot). I walk into the kitchen feeling like a little kid again: scared, not sure what to do.

So much for everything being fine.

Mami, holding the pink *Q* folder, quickly whirls around and smiles for me. "Happy first day of high school!"

Papi kisses us both, his mustache and goatee itchy but warm against my cheek. He goes to the stove.

There are tears in my mom's eyes. She removes her red-framed glasses and wipes them hard as if they are to blame for her tears. I try to think of something to say to make her feel better, but nothing comes, so I just smile back at her.

"You know," I say after a bit, "I don't need that new skateboard for my birthday."

"Why not?" she asks and pulls the *quince* invitations and envelopes from the pink folder.

"My board is fine." I lean against the kitchen wall.

My mother stares at me suspiciously. "You've done nothing but talk about that board for a year. Is this your sister's idea, too?"

"No, I changed my mind."

"But we want to get you something," my dad insists.

"My *quince* is enough. And I don't need live music for it, either. I really don't."

My mother kisses me. "Everything is going to work out. Don't you worry."

Then she starts driving me nuts with more details about the party, how I still have to address the envelopes after school today and how she wants me to have Yasmin Hernandez as one of my *damas*.

America shuffles into the kitchen, looking like something Natasha dragged out from under the sofa.

My mom snatches up her pink folder.

"Destiny's bad dreams keep interfering with my beauty rest," America moans.

Blocking America's view, my mom hands me a slip of paper behind her back.

"What're you doing?" asks America, who misses nothing.

"My business," my mother replies.

But America runs around my mother and snatches the paper out of my hands. She reads it aloud: "Roses. Tables. Town car. *Damas. Chambelane*s. Dancing lessons. Heels. Choose live band. Destiny's escort? Nicolas Hernandez? Omar Castillo?"

My sister narrows her eyes. "No town car. No live band. No *caballero*."

"We'll see." My mother heads over to the coffeemaker and piles in the scoops.

"What's that supposed to mean?"

"*Vamos a ver*," my mom says. "That's all. We'll see."

America looks at my dad and me. We both shrug.

I finish breakfast, help wash the dishes, kiss everybody good-bye, *muchas gracias* and *adiós*, while my mom and sister start "negotiating" the details of my *quince* again. I grab my book bag as fast as I can and meet up outside with Erin, who lives in a fancy doorman building across the street from me. Then we go and meet up with Stephanie, who lives in a fancy doorman building around the corner.

I guess you could say I live *with* a fancy doorman. But without a rent-stabilized apartment we'd never be able to live on the Upper West Side, and now the rent is late, and my dad might have to work day and night like a slave, and my *quince* sucks because it's making everything worse. Then there's Skate15. No way am I going to mention that to Stephanie and Erin. I know them too well. Erin will make fun of the whole boy thing, and Stephanie will make a big love-connection deal out of it, and I'll end up totally confused. I'm in high school now, and I have to start making up my own mind about boys, right? I still have to text Nicolas back. But what *should* I say? I mean, we only met once, and he's like totally gaga over me. I guess I don't know my own strength. Spider legs don't fail me now! Ha!

I just have to think of something to say that won't make me sound like a dork. If I keep waiting to text back maybe he'll think I'm playing it cool . . . or maybe he'll realize that I am, in fact, a dweeb.

I'm quiet on our ten-minute walk to school, hoping my head doesn't explode from all these thoughts.

As we pass a swarm of cars, trucks, and yellow cabs on 96th Street, Stephanie stops, waves her hand in front of my eyes, and asks, "What's up, *la* woman?"

Stephanie looks amazing as always, wearing seashells in her braided hair, a black tank top, white skinny jeans, and black flats along with those big, dark sunglasses.

She asks, "Are you upset about the whatchamacallit?"

Erin bounces her basketball. "Not that whatchamacallit again. The *cuba-lero*?" She has on dark blue sweatpants and a gray hoodie. Her short brown hair is uncombed, and she's carrying an enormous gym bag across her shoulders. But that's who she is, and the look works on her.

I don't know why it bothers me so much that my friends don't use the word *quinceañera* and mispronounce *caballero*, but it does.

"I'm fine," I say, grabbing Erin's basketball.

Stephanie points at her flats. "Aren't these great? They were only a hundred bucks."

Only a hundred bucks? They really don't get it.

We start walking again, and Erin snatches her ball back. "I got season tickets to the Liberty games! You guys can come with me when my dad can't."

"Uh," says Stephanie. "No thanks. I'm going to join the Museum of Modern Art. It's only fifty dollars. You guys want to join?"

"I'll ask my parents," I say. But I won't.

"Listen to this." Stephanie gives me one of the ear buds from her iPod. "It's Beyoncé's latest. You should get one for your birthday," she says. "And stop sharing your sister's iPod."

"C'mon." Erin pats me on the back. "What's up with your face? It's more stressed out than usual."

"I'm slowly being torn in two by family, that's all." I groan. "My mother and sister are still fighting over my *quince*. It's a stupid birthday. Why is everyone flipping out?"

"Yeah," agrees Erin. "No big deal."

"C'mon, Destiny's the first of us turning fifteen. That is a really big deal," says Stephanie. "We have to celebrate!"

"Do you ever think sometimes it'd just be easier to go to sleep and wake up when high school is all over?" I say. "I can't deal with how much my mother and sister are freaking out these days."

"Then don't do that stupid thing," says Erin. "I would have totally refused if my mother tried to get me to do a bat mitzvah."

"I have to do it."

"Her mother will be disappointed if she doesn't," explains Stephanie.

"So let her be." Erin dribbles her basketball. "Life is hard, kid. Get used to it."

I almost snap, "You have no idea," but I don't.

We round the corner at 93rd Street, and my stomach flip-flops.

Columbus Prep is a pretty old school. There's a large modern building attached to a brownstone (the original building) where they put the younger kids. It's two hundred years old or something and was built for boys to prepare them for college. They began letting in girls in the '60s or '70s, and then came scholarship kids, and then there was America and then me. The school is called nonprofit, but even the kindergartners pay thousands of dollars each year (or their parents do). I'd hate to see how much a for-profit school would cost!

As we're walking toward the building, all these guys are staring at Stephanie, and I want to scream, "Hey, I'm here, too!"

Yasmin Hernandez and her friends Melanie and Amanda are sitting on one of the long rows of steps. Yasmin is curvy with freckles and a bright blue streak in her shoulder-length reddish hair. She's wearing a tight Boy Scout shirt that makes her boobs look huge, a Catholic school skirt, and a baseball cap that says Just Do It. For a second, I almost wish we were one of those schools with uniforms. Almost.

Yasmin wasn't always like this. She's really changed. She also wears contacts now and her fingernails are bright red and there's a little heart tattoo on her ankle, which I have to admit is kind of pretty. She didn't always hang out with Melanie and Amanda, either.

I remember the old Yasmin. Everyone used to make fun of her. It was nothing she did, really. Maybe because she was a little too tall like me, too pale, and too whiny with scraped knees and her glasses all crooked. Okay, she was a mess. It's good that she's grown out of her awkward phase, but at the same time, I kind of miss the old Yasmin. I've always been one for the underdog. I invited her to my birthday party in seventh grade, and because of that, some girls didn't come. (Erin and Stephanie did, and the three of us have been best friends ever since.)

Then Yasmin spent the summer after seventh with her relatives in Miami and came back a hottie. Can you spell T-o-t-a-l M-a-k-e-o-v-e-r?

I don't want to stop to say hello, but Yasmin waves me over, and I feel like I shouldn't be cold or rude because our parents have known each other for so many years. They all grew up together in Puerto Rico.

So I stop.

Stephanie and Erin keep going. Erin can't stand anything about Yasmin now. Stephanie likes her new clothes but hates her new friends.

Amanda and Melanie are wearing matching pink velvet tracksuits. Amanda is a skinny blonde, and Melanie is a skinny brunette. Amanda's father owns some huge pizza chain dynasty in Long Island, and she gets free pizza for her friends whenever she wants. Melanie's family makes a fortune selling furniture. Everything about them, especially their matching

Juicy Couture bags and pink, light-up cell phones, annoys me.

It seems as if Yasmin and her girls are real buddy-buddy, but I know they used to rip Yasmin apart every chance they got. Now that Yasmin gets lots of attention from guys, I guess she's okay to hang out with, which is pretty messed up if you ask me. Amanda and Melanie are phonies. Fakes. Users. Abusers. Period. I don't think they're real about anything or care about anybody. Except themselves. I'd hate to be like that. I really would.

But I start thinking, why would Nicolas Hernandez ever want me when he probably already has a hot skinny girlfriend in a pink velvet tracksuit?

"I was telling Amanda and Melanie about Florida," says Yasmin. She gets up from the stairs and goes on and on about how she got to spend another summer in Miami, one of the gifts for her *quince*, and I admit I'm a little jealous. Even though everything about Yasmin annoys me now: how she talks, how she stands, how she shifts her weight from leg to leg to make sure her butt really jiggles and sticks out for the boys to notice.

"I met this guy named Julio," Yasmin continues and shows us his picture on her phone. "He's really sexy, and we're totally in love, and he's going to visit me during winter break."

Amanda cracks her gum as she checks out the picture. "He's pretty cute."

He is. He has long hair that falls into his eyes, like Nicolas, except his hair is really dark, and he's smiling in a goofy way that Nicolas probably never would.

Why am I thinking about Nicolas so much?

"Yeah," agrees Yasmin, gazing at the picture of Julio. "We had this instant connection, you know? He totally gets who I am without me having to explain it."

Why can't that happen to me? I did meet Nicolas, though. If only he'd ask to be my escort to the *quince*. If I'm *allowed* to have an escort? Why didn't I text Nicolas back right away? Why is everything so messed up? Why doesn't he ask me already? Why? Why? Why? Why is the sky blue?

"What?" says Amanda.

"What?" I echo.

"You just said, 'Why is the sky blue?'" Melanie tells me.

Melanie and Amanda laugh in unison, like two pink hyenas.

"Oh." I can't believe I said that out loud!

"She was thinking." Yasmin claps me on the shoulder. "You should try it sometime."

"Oooh." Amanda crosses her arms, but she looks a little hurt.

"Oooh," Melanie repeats.

"I'm sorry if I'm not smart enough for you," Amanda says. "Maybe you should, like, tutor me or something since I'm such a moron."

"I was only joking," says Yasmin and tugs at the sleeve of Amanda's tracksuit.

Amanda shakes her blonde head, gives Yasmin a "whatever" look, and strolls into school. Melanie follows her. Yasmin is quiet for a moment as if she feels guilty. Then she asks me, "So, are you going to have your *quince* at Tavern on the Green?"

Like I said, the Hernandez family is R-I-C-H, even by

Columbus Prep standards. Yasmin's two older brothers are computer geniuses and have their own company in Miami. They threw that huge *quince* at Tavern on the Green in Central Park with crystal and linen and flowers everywhere. Yasmin wore a white Cinderella dress and a tiara, and at the end of the party, her brothers gave her a diamond necklace in the shape of her name and a red Corvette! She can't even drive yet! I have to say she looked beautiful, and the car thing was insane. Yasmin's living *la vida* MTV. My mom said they were planning it for two years, and the whole thing cost over one hundred thousand dollars! I just sat back and watched everybody dancing and eating and being fake. I only went because my parents made me, since the Hernandezes are "like family," which is a really scary thought. Yasmin's mom is more fake than Amanda and Melanie put together.

"Okay," I tell Yasmin, "if you'll pay for me to have my *quince* at Tavern on the Green, I will."

Yasmin, who has probably been to Tavern about a thousand times and never thought twice about it, gets all red and stumbles on, "Well, the vibe at Tavern's not really my thing either, and . . . I guess you're right. . . . Um . . . I should find Amanda and apologize. . . . I'll see you later. . . . I didn't mean to—"

Before she can finish, two older boys I don't know come over, and one of them puts his arm around her waist. The other boy yells, "You have a big ass!"

Yasmin laughs like that's a great compliment, and the three of them head up the steps.

I pretend to be checking my schedule. How can I begin

to worry about my *quinceañera*? High school is enough of a problem! I don't have my mom or America taking charge here. I almost wish I did. But Mami's safe at work and America's off with the seniors doing senior stuff, and I'm standing here with my own problems.

Alone.

2 minutes later

HIGH SCHOOL

It's both nice and really nerve-wracking to see all these familiar faces at school and a lot of faces that aren't at all familiar. I think my legs are longer than they were last night, and five new pimples sprung up on the walk over. Everyone seems so much older and cooler this year, except me. New students, new teachers, new advisor, same building but now I get to use the cafeteria reserved for 9th–12th graders. I'm movin' on up!

Or am I? I head to the basement, find my locker, and put my new lock on it. Yasmin's a few lockers away with "you-have-a-big-ass" boy. He's practically on top of her.

1st Period

English. Our reading list is longer than my legs! Combined! When the bell rings, I hook up with Erin and Stephanie in the hallway. I'm a little upset that I don't have any classes with them, but when I run into them in the hall, we hug and give each other a kiss. I really do love my friends. They get me through the rough times. As America puts it, a friend is not someone you use once and throw away—a friend is someone you use again and again and again! Ha.

2nd Period

Spanish. *Yo hablo español. Usted habla español. Él habla español.* I wish my parents spoke more of it at home. I sound like somebody born and raised in Minnesota trying to speak Inuit.

3rd Period

Ceramics. I try to make a deer out of clay, and it comes out looking like an ashtray. Potter's wheel next week.

4th Period

Biology. Classes seem kind of overwhelming so far, especially this one.

5th Period

Gym. Don't ask.

Lunch

One thing that's a major drag is that I don't have the same lunchtime as Stephanie and Erin. The high-school caf is about twice the size of the junior-high caf, and it's pretty intimidating if you don't know anyone. I feel like one of those new girls that I used to feel sorry for, sitting by themselves and hoping someone would join them. Rosie, the perpetually pissed off cashier, is looking like good company!

Then I see Yasmin sitting by herself. She's in the same boat as me.

"Hey!" she calls out as I search for an empty table.

"Hey."

"You can sit here if you want. It's pretty crowded."

So I sit down. We eat, and neither of us says anything, and it's kind of awkward. Without thinking, I blurt out, "How're things going with you and your cousin Nicolas? You know, his staying with you and everything?"

I guess I'm hoping she'll say how crazy Nicolas is about me after only meeting me once and how he can't sleep or eat or concentrate on anything, but she just shrugs, and says, "Okay, I guess."

It's back to awkward silence after that, but I sort of dig her courage in calling me over. Sometimes it's a relief to sit with someone and not have to say anything.

"Uh, what kind of meat do you think this is?" she asks me after a while, holding open the bun on her cheeseburger. Not batting an eye, I reply, "I don't know, but my cat, Natasha, went missing this morning. . . ."

She laughs. I do, too.

6th Period

Geometry. Somebody, hit me on the head with a rock! *Please.*

7th Period

US History. Mr. Diamant, besides being the funniest person I think I've ever met, is such a cool teacher. America had him, too. He likes to act out the parts of historical figures and has no shame about jumping up on the desk to illustrate how Abraham Lincoln gave public speeches or how Harriet Tubman ran away to the North. Instead of term papers, we'll get to do projects like writing letters between two historical figures:

"Dear Harriet, keep up the great work! You are so cool! Love, Abe."

Neat, huh? (I am such a nerd!) My real ones will be a lot better.

8th Period

Drama. Why drama? I'm not an actress, but I saw the description "increases sense of confidence" on the list of class choices, and I picked it. What could be so bad about increasing confidence?

Drama's held in the school theater, and it's empty when I get there. I sit in the second row.

Yasmin comes in and sits down next to me. I guess she's trying to find confidence, too? And an easy class.

"So you're interested in drama?" she asks.

"No, I'm just doing this class for fun." I fumble with my book bag.

I almost hit the deck when I spot Amanda strolling in with Melanie. They pick seats in the back of the theater.

"Oh . . . I should probably go. . . ." Yasmin gets up and joins them.

The rest of the class files in, and then Mr. Porton bounces in last with a bag slung across his shoulder. He seems kind of young and old all at once. With bright red hair and a matching red beard, short with a big belly, he's like a redheaded Santa. He takes attendance at the desk to the side of the stage and then hops onto the stage and grins at us.

"Greetings, fellow thespians! Welcome to drama!" Mr. Porton bows a little. He reaches into his shoulder bag and pulls out a stack of papers, which he fans out on the edge of the stage.

"Okay, you guys, come on up." He points at the papers. "You'll notice a character name at the top of these scenes and a brief description of who they are and what their monologue is about. Don't think about it too much. Pick the first one that grabs you! Or vice versa. Tomorrow we'll have everyone come up and read aloud. Sound good?"

Everyone nods reluctantly. Then we trudge up to the stage and sift through the monologues. There are all these characters I've never heard of, and nothing even remotely resembles anything that I could read out loud without sounding like a complete idiot. I think this class might be a mistake. Yasmin comes over to me again.

"Feeling a little lost?" she says.

"Yeah" is all I can manage.

She searches through the monologues, pulls one out, and hands it to me. "How about this?"

It's Juliet. Freaking Shakespeare!

"Thanks," I say.

"It's such an awesome play, and Juliet's a lot stronger than most people give her credit for. She totally defies her parents and is willing to risk death to be with this guy she really loves. She's—"

Amanda and Melanie come over, and Yasmin goes quiet.

"This class totally blows!" exclaims Amanda.

"Yeah, and what's up with that man-purse Mr. Porton's carrying?" Melanie snorts.

Amanda twirls one finger through her perfect blonde hair, like she's bored with this conversation. Then she grabs a sheet of paper without even looking at it. "C'mon, let's go read these stupid things and get this class over with already."

She and Melanie bop back toward their seats. Yasmin starts to follow them, then turns to me for a second like she's going to say something—maybe invite me to join them?—but thinks better of it and turns back, following behind Melanie and Amanda without another word about Romeo or Juliet.

2:55 p.m.

Phew! My first day is over. I exit the building in a horde of kids and instead of taking my usual route home, I head in the opposite direction, thinking about how I'm all turned around on the inside, too. I wish Erin wasn't at basketball practice and Stephanie wasn't at modern dance class. I cross the street and hear, "Yo, *chica*, where's your board?"

I look and there's Nicolas, holding a slice of pizza.

"Where's yours?" I ask as casually as I can.

He motions to his backpack, and there's his skateboard sticking out. He's looking really cute in baggy jeans and a black *Watchmen* T-shirt. When he takes a huge bite out of his slice, he's totally oblivious to the grease that's dribbled down his chin. If anyone can pull off a greasy chin, it's definitely Nicolas. "I met your mom," he says. "She's a talker."

"You met my mother?"

"Yeah. She was at my aunt's house telling us about your *quinceañera*."

When did she do that? How could she have? Unless it was . . . right after . . . *flan*! Wow! My mother is magical. That lady works fast. Worlds are colliding! The end is near!

Nicolas gives me this intense gaze, and I'm totally waiting for him to confess that he's Skate15.

His phone beeps. It's a text, which he reads, and he smiles as he texts back. When he's done, he glances at me, but it's not intense like a moment ago. It's kind of absent, like he's already gone.

"I gotta meet up with Yasmin and her girlfriends," he says. "Then I gotta get home and start writing a paper about the Harlem Renaissance. Giving us a paper on the first day of school. You believe that?"

"Oh, yeah. That sucks."

"See ya."

And then he's gone. Oh my God! Did my mother ask him to be my *caballero*? No, she wouldn't. That would be *so* humiliating.

I was hoping to start high school with as little drama as possible. Focus on my classes (okay, one of them *is* drama), my board, maybe a boyfriend (okay, that might involve some drama, too). I think everybody in the world should just take a deep breath and slow down. Everything's changing so fast that all I want to do when I get home is watch TV, snuggle with Natasha, and ask my teddy bear, Fuzzy, what he knows about geometry. Stop the ride! I want to get off!

Instead, as soon as I walk through the door, my mom shouts, "Destiny! They're waiting for you!"

Not even a "How was your first day, *mija*?"

"What're you doing home from work so early?" I ask.

We have extra bills to pay and she's cutting work hours? Why do I suddenly feel like the parent around here?

"It's a surprise for your *quince*!"

Oh no. Not again.

LOS GUAPOS

I used to love this book about a boy who finds a red balloon, and the balloon refuses to leave his side and waits for him no matter where he goes. I think my mother is becoming my red balloon. . . .

I walk into the living room (followed by my balloon) and there they are, guitars and drums set up like they're about to give a concert. Natasha, relaxing on the coffee table, stares up at me with cool blue eyes.

"Surprise!" says my mother, as if she needs to repeat the concept. "This is the band I've chosen for your *quinceañera*!"

It's *Los Guapos*! America's ex, Tomas (lead singer and guitar), is wearing an American flag shirt over faded jeans with a Cuban flag bandana tied around his spiky black hair. Hailey's boyfriend, Kyle (drums), has the same shirt but with an Irish flag around his long red hair. Maritza's boyfriend, Byron (bass player and backup vocals), wears his American flag shirt with a Haitian bandana. Very "We Are the World." They look as good as their name—The Handsome Ones.

"One. Two. Three. Four." Tomas starts singing, "I lost my heart in *Nueva* York . . ."

And God, he sounds good, too.

Fact check: I used to tag along with America, Maritza, and Hailey to watch *Los Guapos* play around the city at different high-school dances. We would boogie to every song (including such hits as "My *Corazón*," "Don't Leave, *Amor*," and "I *Quiero* You"). *Los Guapos* totally rock, kind of like The Beatles meets Los Lonely Boys.

Tomas and America went out all during eleventh (he was her first boyfriend), and she made it a point not to become what she calls "a stupid girl." You know, the girls that spend all their time with their boyfriends, forgetting their friends and their goals and their dreams and stuff like that. As *Los Guapos* became more and more popular, Tomas changed. The last time we went to see them in June, he was surrounded by all these groupie chicks in microminis and tube tops who took our places by the front of the stage. Then, after the show, America caught Tomas making out backstage with some stupid girl he used to go out with in tenth.

America freaked out and broke up with him but then spent her time obsessing about why he cheated on her. She almost couldn't study for her final exams. It was spooky to see my sister that powerless, and I was so glad when she snapped out of it. She began working with Planned Parenthood and fighting harder for women's rights. But secretly I missed Tomas and the band. And I think America did, too.

And now here they are again. *Los Guapos*. Live in my living room. And my mom and I are like a couple of those groupie chicks parked in front of Tomas as he strums hard on his guitar.

Tomas is a cutie (did I mention that?), and my mother

loves him because he's ambitious and talented and most of all because America never told her about that stupid girl. If Mami ever found out that Tomas cheated on her daughter, she would completely disown him. But she still thinks the breakup was all America's fault and Tomas is a sweet angel with a golden voice.

I don't understand why my sister never told her the truth. All America said was, "We're too different." It's like she's trying to protect Tomas or something. Like she doesn't want my mom to think badly of him. Watching my mother snap her fingers offbeat as Tomas's throaty voice fills the air with "*Corazón, my Corazón,*" I start to get angry about the whole thing. Sometimes I think boys just want a stupid girl. I don't think I'm a stupid girl, but I might want to spend a little time with a boy like Nicolas. So what does that say about me?

"Destiny!"

The music stops.

I look behind me, and there's America in her softball uniform, patches of grass stains and dirt on her knees, a disgusted expression on her face.

"HOW COULD YOU?" Then she shouts at Tomas, "Do you remember that time you got kicked in the balls?"

"Uh, no."

"That's right," says America. "I'm actually talking to you from the future."

Tomas lowers his guitar for protection. The other guys laugh nervously.

"Get out of my apartment!" she yells. "All three of you!"

"America!" my mother scolds. "Don't be rude."

"This is a total invasion of my privacy!" America throws her softball glove at Tomas, who ducks. It lands too close to Natasha. She hisses at all of us and runs off to hide under my bed. I wish I could join her.

"A 'How are you?' would be nice," says Tomas, and he actually dares to smile at America. "Or, 'Long time no see.'"

"Not long enough," she replies.

"America," my mother scolds again, "Tomas is here as my guest. Where are your manners?"

"He's *my* ex-boyfriend!"

My mother shakes her head and sighs. She thinks my sister dumped Tomas for no good reason and here he is, willing to help us out and play music for my *quince*, so why is America being so hard on him? I feel bad that my mother doesn't know the truth, and I almost feel like telling her, but I can't—that's my sister's job. And it doesn't seem like she'll be doing it anytime soon.

TV, anyone?

"Destiny needs a band for her *quince*," says my mom. "And now she has one. They've offered to play for free! Isn't that wonderful? Tomas wants you to come, and he wants to be a *chambelán*. Right, Tomas?"

"Yeah," he says. "It'll be cool."

I smile at his enthusiasm. I can't help it.

America glares at me and sighs even more dramatically than my mother. "Now I'm really glad I'm not going!"

My mother sniffles and tries to force herself to cry, but nothing comes. I play along and pat her shoulder. "Good try."

"*Gracias,*" says my mother, facing America. "What about

all the sacrifices I make for you? Going without food when times were hard so that you could eat?"

"I don't think the bathroom scale would agree with that story."

My mom gasps and pulls in her belly.

I bite my tongue so I won't laugh.

"Is that why we send you to school? To use your education against your mother?"

"Send me? What am I, a postcard?"

Los Guapos go from amused to really uncomfortable. After all, they came to surprise me and play music, not become part of The Ringling Lozada Family Circus.

"Hey, maybe we should split, Tomas," says Kyle.

"Excellent idea," agrees America. "Don't let the door hit you where the Good Lord split you!"

Byron and Kyle pack up and leave as fast as they can, but Tomas stays behind, staring at America with puppy-dog eyes.

"Tomas is practically family," my mother protests. "Of course, we will use his band. I won't argue about this anymore, America. I have been planning Destiny's *quinceañera* for years."

"You've been planning it since July!"

"In my heart," my mother declares and pats her chest. "I've been planning it in my heart."

"That's it! I'm moving out! Where is my suitcase?" America shouts.

"Again?" my mother says.

"Shhh, America, give it a rest," says Tomas.

Bad idea.

America and my mom (who doesn't like anybody shushing America but her) both shoot Tomas a look that would knock the needles off a Christmas tree.

Tomas shuts up. Fast.

America marches out of the room and my mother chases after her, pleading in Spanish that she's only trying to make everybody happy and why can't America understand that, all the way down the hall until we hear two doors slam and the world goes quiet.

"So?" Tomas strums a lick on his guitar. "Did we pass the audition?"

TOMAS LOVES AMERICA

The good news is, my mom was so distracted by *Los Guapos* that she forgot all about my having to stuff and address my *quince* invitations. The bad news is, after Tomas leaves, I go into our room, and America is talking on her cell phone and packing her giant suitcase. We have twin beds on opposite sides of the room, two tall shelves lined with books, a small TV on my dresser, and a shared desk and computer in front of a long window. America has a Rosie the Riveter "We Can Do It!" poster on the wall by her bed. There's a clipping of a Plan B Rodriguez Super Future Deck on the wall above mine. I've been dreaming of getting the Super Future for my birthday since long before this *quince* stuff started. It costs about $150 (for the deck, wheels, trucks, bearings, risers, grip tape, and hardware, and then you have to put it all together) and it's really, really cool. It's got all these hazy, swirling colors on it that look kind of like planets colliding.

"I'm so sick of this *quince* stuff!" America tosses her cell on her bed.

"Me, too." I put on my Yankees cap and throw myself on my bed.

"She has the nerve to go behind my back and book *Los*

Guapos? That's . . . downright illegal!"

"Illegal?"

"It should be. I'm suing. I'm suing everybody. Mami, Papi, you!"

"Me?" I hoped I was safe here. Ignored but safe.

"I saw the expression on your face when I came in. You were totally into *Los Guapos.*"

I don't know what to say to that.

"So you're on her side now?" America asks.

"I'm not on anyone's side. Look, Mami always liked Tomas. She *still* likes Tomas, because you never told her what happened. Maybe because . . . you wanted a chance to get back with him?" There, I said it.

"Say what?" America puts her hands on her hips.

"Um . . ." I chicken out. "*Los Guapos* are going to play for free, and you said Mami and Papi can't afford a band, so it all works out."

America snorts and returns to folding her Girl Power T-shirts.

"Where are you going?"

"To stay with Hailey until Mami signs off on your demands. She and Maritza are on their way over."

I'm afraid to say anything else. America leaves to go to the bathroom. Natasha jumps up on my bed. She yawns and circles my lap, then finally decides that my shoulder is a good place to sit. I cuddle Fuzzy so he won't get jealous.

Soon Maritza pokes her pink head through the door. She and Hailey tiptoe in like they're guilty of something and trying not to get caught.

Maritza whispers, "Shut the door."

Hailey shuts it and leans back to block anyone from coming in.

"What's up?" I ask.

"Tomas," says Hailey. "While we don't excuse his behavior, we believe he made a mistake and he's sorry."

"And he totally loves America," says Maritza.

"Tomas hasn't been with anybody else since they broke up," adds Hailey. "Kyle and Byron say he's miserable."

"And America is miserable, too. We're getting them back together." Maritza sits at the edge of my bed.

"If America finds out," I tell them, "she's going to kill you both."

"It's already killing us trying to keep Tomas away from America," says Hailey.

"When we go out with the guys, we can't be with the two of them." Maritza grabs Fuzzy from my lap and squeezes him for support. "It makes everybody miserable."

"It was our idea for *Los Guapos* to offer to play for free at your *quince*," admits Maritza. "Don't tell your mom."

"No!" I rescue Fuzzy from her clutches.

"Shhh." Hailey puts a finger in front of her lips.

"You guys are total double-crossers."

"But it's for the greater good," insists Maritza. "America misses Tomas as much as he misses her. We've all been punished enough."

"We want America to be happy," says Hailey, "which is why we're going to leave here and *conveniently* run into Tomas on the way back to my place. He's going to convince America, once and for all, that they should get back together and that he won't ever let anything like that happen again."

I gently nudge Natasha off my shoulder and slump back against the wall.

Maritza bends toward me. "What do you think?"

I think they have completely lost their minds. Before I can answer, there's a thumping noise at the door.

"Destiny!" America calls. "The door is stuck again!"

Hailey hesitates, then jumps away from the door and grabs Natasha, pretending to listen to her heart. Maritza pulls a notepad from her bag and leafs through it with exaggerated concentration.

America stumbles in and regards us suspiciously.

Hailey and Maritza exchange glances. I tug my baseball cap low.

"Ready to go?" asks Hailey.

"Almost." America goes back to packing.

Maritza gets this strange expression on her face. Rated C for Coo-Coo. "I just had an idea," she says. "What if you get *Los Guapos* to play the music you want at Destiny's *quince*? Turn it into an Anti-*quince*?"

Hailey claps. "That's it! They can play loud, antisocial, angry music. Like The Sex Pistols and Green Day."

America thinks about it. She nods slowly, grins, grabs a short black skirt and black combat boots out of the pile on her bed, slaps on some red lipstick, and is out the door with The Jezebels before I can say, *21st Century Breakdown*.

At 9:30 p.m., I'm sitting on my bed, finishing my homework and getting advice from Fuzzy and Natasha on whether or not

I should text Skate15. (Natasha says yes; Fuzzy says that I should hibernate on it and eat more fish.)

America bursts in and announces, "I'm back with Tomas!"

I act surprised. "What? Why?"

"Because he's obviously still in love with me. That's why he came here today. Not because of Mami or the *quince* but because of me. Hailey, Maritza, and I went searching for Tomas and ran into him before we got past Amsterdam, and he asked me if we could go somewhere alone. He apologized again. I realized tonight that he really means it and that I still want to be with him. We took a walk in Riverside Park and talked and talked and looked out at the Hudson River. God, it felt so good, you know? He really does understand me better than anyone."

"So, you were in the park all this time?"

(Fact: America is not a virgin. If the twenty-five hundred SAFE SEX and WEAR CONDOMS buttons that she pins on her bag don't give that away.)

"I don't need to stay at Hailey's now," she says, avoiding my question.

"I'm glad you and Tomas are back together," I say carefully. I feel guilty, but glad, because she seems happy. "So *Los Guapos* are going to play at my *quince?*"

"Of course they are. I'm your older sister, Dusty. I'm here to help."

"Should we go tell Mami the good news about you and Tomas?"

America grins. "Yes! But first!" She places a sheet of lined paper with scribbling on it down on my bed.

"What's this?"

"A list of new songs that Tomas is writing for your *quince*. I helped him think of the names."

I pick up the list. It goes on and on. Real subtle titles like, "Stop Trying to Ruin My *Vida!*" The kind of spirit that brings a family together.

"I did miss Tomas," admits America. "I guess I can thank Mami for this."

And The Jezebels, I think.

"But we're going to turn this *quince* thing inside out, Dusty!"

I nod my head like it's all okay with me. I wouldn't mind so much if America helped with the music for my *quince*, and it's going to save money, but now we're back to a tug-of-war with my mom, where nobody seems to win.

America kisses my cheek. "I'm going to add the new songs to your list of demands."

"Great," I say.

She bounces out of the room. I go on the computer to see if I can find anything on YouTube to inspire me for my Juliet monologue tomorrow. I don't find anything useful, but I'm watching a hilarious video by Flight of the Concords about "Albi the Racist Dragon" when Nicolas pops up in an IM. He probably got my IM from Omar! Man, Nicolas is nuts about me! I must learn to use my powers wisely. Ha!

Skate15: hey there. what's up? why didn't u txt me back?

I freeze. My heart is beating hard. My throat gets dry. I almost don't want to answer. What's wrong with me? Write back this time! Just do it, Destiny.

DLo: Hey. Was totally going to text you back. How are you?

Skate15: i had one of those kinda days, could use some company.

DLo: What kinda day?

Skate15: the kind where u open ur eyes & u know u shoulda kept em closed!

DLo: Yeah, I know those days, been having a lot of them lately.

Skate15: no more frosted flakes left this morning so i had to eat cheerios. then i tried to ride my board 2 school but the front wheels r loose so i gotta bring it in, which BLOWS. everyone at skool getting on my nerves & it's only the 1st day, y'know?

DLo: Totally. My mom and sis are driving me INSANE with all this quince stuff & then there's the whole caballero thing. Don't get me going on that!

I hit send and then I worry, should I have mentioned the *caballero*? What will he say? Does it look like I'm trying too hard?

Skate15: a caballero, huh?

He's not biting yet. But it can't hurt to keep trying?

DLo: My mom says why bother having a quince @ all if I don't get escorted by a nice young man (her words, not mine). Maybe she has a point and I should call the whole thing off. Ha! My sis doesn't want me to have a caballero and they're fighting WWIII over it and I swear sometimes it's like they're loving every minute of it!

Skate15: why doesn't ur sis want u 2 have a caballero?

92

DLo: She says it's all phony, so why should some random boy (her words, not mine) walk in with me on his arm? I think it's because she has issues with her ex who she just got back 2gether with 2night and is taking it out on my quince.

Skate15: what if the caballero was your boyfriend?

(Is he asking me what I think he's asking me?)

Skate15: u still there?

DLo: Yup.

Skate15: do u have a boyfriend?

DLo: Only 1. He lives under my bed and he's imaginary.

Skate15: hehe. i'm jealous.

I can't tell if he's joking because I'm joking—but if he's not joking, I'm about to freak out!

DLo: I guess if I had a boyfriend, it might be different.

Skate15: did u ever?

DLo: Ever what?

Skate15: have a boyfriend!

DLo: Why u asking? Did u ever have a girlfriend?

Skate15: sure. tons! i got six hanging all over me as i type this. u?

DLo: I guess I did. Sorta. Maybe not technically.

Skate15: hmm, what does "not technically" mean?

DLo: Nothing 2 serious. U know.

Skate5: um . . . not sure I do. explain, please.

DLo: There was this guy I used 2 hang with last year.

Skate15: did u guys ever make out?

DLo: I'm not going 2 give you any of the gory details!

Skate15: aha! so there r gory details?

DLo: Maybe. A few.

Skate15: that's enuf. u don't need 2 tell me.

DLo: Gee, thanks.

Skate15: but was it exciting?

DLo: Kind of. I wished I would have been more into him, tho. He wasn't 2 exciting, no mystery.

Skate15: so with someone ur into, u like 4 there 2 b mystery?

DLo: I guess.

Skate15: do u like knowing that someone likes u or not really being sure?

DLo: Mystery is good but if he likes me, would b nice 2 let me know for sure some day!

Skate15: man, girls have it easy!

DLo: How do u figure that??

Skate15: u sit back & let us do all the work, make all the moves.

DLo: What moves?

Skate15: u saying u want me to make a move?

DLo: U saying u want 2?

(Oh no! Too much?)

DLo: Still there?

Skate15: yup. well, maybe ur wish will come true.

DLo: Maybe. . . .

Skate15: i should go. i have to download some stuff for an essay. thanx for the chitty-chat.

DLo: Any time.

Skate15: yeah?

DLo: Yeah.

Skate15: see ya.

DLo: See ya?

But he's already signed off and just like that, Nicolas is gone again. I save our IM, print it out, and read it over and over. He's going to make a move! There's nothing America can do to stop that, and maybe she won't make trouble once it's set.

He's going to ask to be my *caballero* any minute now. I know it.

All I have to do is wait. . . .

2nd day of high school: friday

LENNY AND THE KISS

As I'm heading to the kitchen for breakfast, I pass my parents' room, where my dad's finishing up his morning push-ups and sit-ups while my mom's on the treadmill. She's wearing a yellow leotard (like a giant banana) and when she spots me, she calls out, "*Los Guapos* are playing at your *quince*! My plan worked! It's only a matter of time before I convince your sister to go! And you still have to address the envelopes!"

I nod. My dad nods, too, and follows me into the kitchen. I hear the treadmill switch off, and soon Mami's standing next to my dad at the stove, singing, "*Que será será*," as I set the table. They're still sweaty from their workouts, and the September heat that fills the kitchen doesn't help. I'm not too proud to say my parents are in need of a shower and some deodorant. *Pronto.*

My mother hits brew on the coffeemaker and asks me, "Aren't you happy about *Los Guapos*?"

"What about the *quince* demands?" I reply. I think about asking, What about the rent? But one problem at a time, *por favor*.

"Your sister and I are negotiating," says my mother with a smile and a wink. She gulps down some vitamins with a glass of water and gets out the two blue coffee mugs.

My dad grabs a stack of bread out of the breadbox.

"Your father's making French toast," my mom announces, handing him some cinnamon from the cupboard.

"Good morning!" America comes in with a notebook, a physics textbook, and a pencil. My mother practically attacks her, hugging her so tight that my sister's eyes pop. She coos, "Good morning, my little angel."

"Mom!"

After my mother releases her, America lays her stuff down on the table, and goes to the cupboard.

"Hey, we're out of Fancy Feast again!"

"It's okay, she can eat regular tuna fish," my mom tells America.

I look down at Natasha, who is glaring up at my sister. America scoops tuna fish into a large cat bowl and places it on the floor. Natasha takes one whiff and walks away in disgust. Not fancy enough. *Madame* Natasha has left the building.

"I want everybody to know," America announces, "that after breakfast I'd like to hold a family meeting about the *quince* and *Los Guapos* and exactly how much everything is going to change."

My mother's face drops. "Don't start, America."

My father combines milk, eggs, and cinnamon in a plastic bowl. "America, please. Just one morning of peace."

America begins, "I'm only trying to—"

My mother grabs a piece of bread and shoves it into my sister's mouth. America chews and grumbles, "Hilarious."

My father greases a pan with butter. But I can tell he's worried. I know my parents pretty well.

I'm going to say something. . . .

"Destiny?"

I look at my mother.

"You're just standing there staring at your father."

"Thinking," I say.

"About your *quince*?" My mother's all happy. "Thinking about how your father is so proud of you?"

"Are you proud of me, Papi?" I ask as he dips a piece of bread into the plastic bowl.

"Always." My father places the first slice of drippy bread on the sizzling pan.

"Are you proud of me, too?" asks America, sitting next to me at the table and cracking open her physics textbook.

"You," says my father, "not so much."

"Then why'd you have me?" America grins.

"Tax deduction," says my mom, pouring the coffee.

"And why'd you have Destiny?"

"We thought we'd get lucky the second time around." My mom shrugs.

My sister ruffles my hair. "Awwwwww!"

"And we were right," adds my father.

"I want new parents!" America pounds the kitchen table.

"Bring me the forms tomorrow," my mother tells her, smiling. "I will sign those happily. *Vaya con Dios*."

"Have you ever been in love, Mami?" I ask. I don't mean to change the subject, but I can't stop thinking about Nicolas and this whole *caballero* thing.

98

"*Claro.* Of course."

"When?"

"With your father, silly."

"That doesn't count." America looks up from her book. "She means, *really* in love."

"I was in love once with a boy named Lenny in Isabela. Before I met your father. Is that good enough for you?"

"What happened to Lenny?" asks America.

"He was perfect. Beautiful. *Buenísimo*! Nice dresser. And such manners!"

"So what happened?" I ask.

"I was five." My mother comes over to the table. "We shared a cot at naptime, and he pooped in his pants. After that, the magic was gone."

"That's disgusting," says America.

My mother laughs. "The truth is, he just wasn't right for me. He wasn't your father."

"Ah." My father removes the last piece of French toast from the stove, turns off the heat, and asks my mother, "You wouldn't leave me if I pooped in my pants, would you?"

My mom dashes across the kitchen, looks my father in the eye, and declares, "I will never leave you."

He places both hands on his heart. Then he opens his arms wide, and my mom gives him a tight hug. They hold each other until my father says, "Uh, oh . . . honey?"

"What?"

"I think I did a Lenny."

My mother pushes him away. America yells, "Ewwwww!"

"I feel so comfortable with you!" My father chases after

my mother, who shouts, "Get away from me!"

"Hold me!" my father cries as he follows my mom around the kitchen table.

He starts hugging America, saying, "Hold me!" and America jumps up and runs around the kitchen, laughing.

Clowns! My father chases me around the kitchen, too, and I'm laughing and running and laughing and running. . . .

They're clowns, but my parents really are in love and it's actually pretty cool. No money troubles can change that. Maybe Nicolas and I will be high-school sweethearts, just like them. Do guys become your boyfriend if they're already friends with you? My father stops clowning and sets some syrup and a huge plate full of French toast in the middle of the table. I start to dig in when I get a text from Omar:

bunch of us mtg w/ boards in Union sq. @ 5 2day. c u then?

I text him back:

c u then!

I wonder if you-know-who will be there?

I meet up with Stephanie and Erin as usual, and we walk to school. We pass all the kids standing around on the front steps, catching up on the first-day gossip, which music is cool, which YouTube video is dumb, who's in and who's out, who's hot, who's not, who's dopey looking, who's a genius, who's going out with who and reported it on Facebook, who made out with who, who broke up with who and did it on Facebook, who slept with who, who could do better, who's a cool teacher, who's a Nazi.

The morning goes by pretty quickly. In drama class, it's monologue time and Yasmin is seriously kicking ass. She keeps surprising me. Her character is a girl whose father died, and she's at the funeral and doesn't want to see him in the open casket. Even though she's just reading, Yasmin gets really emotional, and I wonder what she's thinking about. When she yells, "I won't! I won't! I won't!" she is so intense and scary that some kids in the audience gasp.

I'm a little mortified that I'm next.

"Okay, Destiny, you're up!" Mr. Porton calls from behind his desk.

I get up from my seat and look around. Everyone's staring at me.

Be cool, I tell myself.

I walk up onto the stage and hold out the monologue to read. My hands are shaking. Is it hot in here? Did someone dim the lights? Is the room spinning?

"Whenever you're ready," Mr. Porton says encouragingly.

I take a deep breath and begin. . . .

"O Romeo, Romeo! Wherefore art thou Romeo? Deny thy father—"

I take a closer look at the paper. What the heck am I saying? I know the monologue is about how Juliet is crawling out of her skin, thinking about Romeo, but the thoughts I have in my head are all about Nicolas, and I can't understand the words on the page. I start pacing back and forth on the stage.

"Uh, Destiny?" Mr. Porton says.

I stop pacing. He thinks I'm horrible. He's throwing me out of his class. "Yes?"

"Quit moving around. Just say the lines."

"Sorry. Can I try again?"

"No problem. Why don't you try it a little more passionately this time?"

"Passionately? Uh, okay."

I say the first few lines again but instead of sounding passionate, I sound whiny.

"I'm no good," I grumble, slapping my legs with the pages.

"Are you kidding? You're doing great," says Mr. Porton.

"You're the teacher. You have to say that."

"No, I don't. You're the one who's brave enough to perform in front of the class."

I scan the room. Amanda and Melanie are snickering. Yasmin gives me an encouraging thumbs up. I can't go on. I shake my head and jump off the stage and sit back down.

I give up.

After school, I try to forget my lousy day. I rush home and spend a couple of hours on my homework. I comb out my hair, but soon I give up on that, too, and put it in a ponytail. I throw on my helmet and pads (just in case Nicolas is there and *insists* I try doing some tricks) and grab my board. I hit the door by 4:30.

I get on my board, kick off, and roll to the subway stop on the corner of 96th and Broadway. I take the train to 14th Street and then skate east to Union Square, where the skateboarders go to roll. There's a farmer's market selling all kinds of fruits and vegetables in that spot every weekend (sometimes America goes with my mom to get fresh stuff for my dad to cook). The rest of the time, it's taken over by skateboarders.

Omar is there with a bunch of kids from his school that I don't know. Nicolas is there, too! I notice that Nicolas kisses a girl with a purple mullet hello, which I'm not too crazy about. But I know it's really hard to resist a girl with a purple mullet, so I stay cool. Still, I feel kind of self-conscious. I just stand there watching.

"Hey." Omar boards toward me.

"Hay is for horses," I say.

Omar makes a horsey noise. "C'mon?"

"What?" I ask. I jump off my board and step down on its tail to flip it up and press it close to my chest.

"Roll, baby, roll," Omar calls out and laughs and rolls away from me. Slowly, I roll after him.

Looking at the Brandeis kids, dressed in black T-shirts and black jeans with silver nose studs and eyebrow rings, you'd think they were really full of themselves, but they turn out to be pretty funny and interesting, even Mullet Girl. I wonder what they thought when they first saw me? Loser probably, holding a board and not skating.

I notice that Nicolas is boarding almost side by side with Mullet Girl.

Does he even know that I'm here?

Finally, I decide it's time to work out all my stress and maybe get Nicolas to notice me. I do some really gross ollies, grinds, and slides. But at least it's good to be doing something, and I feel so free when I'm skating. I forget about Nicolas and Mullet Girl and do a final ollie where I don't actually fall off my board.

"Nice!" says Nicolas, after I land and roll.

I can't believe I did it!

I take a break and sit on the curb.

Nicolas comes over and sits down next to me. I take off my helmet. Is this the moment? Is Skate15 going to ask to be my *caballero*?

"You shouldn't pull your hair back," he says.

Not quite what I was expecting, but I go with it. "I shouldn't?"

"Nah, you should wear it down." He reaches out and touches my hair. "Definitely."

I try to think of something flirty to say, but all I come up with is, "I like your teeth."

"My teeth?"

My face goes hot. "Yeah. . . . They seem really clean."

Nicolas laughs. "Turn around."

"Huh?"

"Turn around. I wanna do something."

The way he says it, so confident that he doesn't have to ask, makes me obey. I'm not sure what I think about that. I feel his fingers on my scrunchie, pulling it down until my hair comes loose.

I turn to him with my long brown hair down.

"Yup, I was right." He smiles. I smile back.

"Can I ask you a question?" I say.

"Maybe." He winks.

"Tell me the truth. Do you have a girlfriend?"

I don't know if I'm light-headed from my first solid ollie or what, but I'm feeling bold for once.

"No girlfriend at this time," he says. "But I'm checking out a couple of applications."

"Are you?" I laugh and push him. "Someone with a nice purple mullet, maybe?"

We sit there smiling again.

"Maybe I should get a purple mullet for my *quince*," I say.

"Hah, I'd like to see that."

This somehow makes me bolder.

"Well, you said you were coming to it, so maybe you will!"

He touches my hair again. "No mullets for you, *quince* Girl. Rock the house with your hair down!"

I'm so knocked out by what he's saying, but I still don't know whether he really plans on coming to my *quince*, let alone whether or not he wants to be my *caballero*. But . . . he must? Otherwise, why would he touch my hair like that?

He moves closer to me, and our shoulders touch. I shiver like it's winter instead of September, like I've rubbed up against Frosty the Snowman. I feel like I'm here alone with Nicolas, even though Omar and a zillion other New Yorkers surround us.

Nicolas frowns. "Your shoulders are all hunched. Turn around again."

Once again, I turn around. I can't help it. He pushes my hair to one side. His hands are warm on my neck. He presses down with his fingers lightly and spreads them to my shoulders, digging in soft but firm.

"Relax," he whispers in my ear. "Take a deep breath and exhale slowly."

I breathe in and then let it go. My shoulders relax and my

head hangs heavy, my chin touching my chest. Nicolas starts rubbing again, and it's kind of painful but at the same time, kind of great. His breath on the back of my neck is cool at first but then goes hot.

"Too much?" he asks.

"Umm-hmm," I murmur. "No. I mean . . . it's nice."

"Good."

I close my eyes. Stephanie would know how to play this moment. She'd smile and toss her head back and tell him . . .

I go blank.

Nicolas runs his fingers through my hair, then to my shoulders again, which gives me goose bumps all up and down my arms.

"Why you so tense?" he asks, his fingers traveling along my spine. As soon as they reach the middle of my back, Omar skates over. I jump up about six hundred feet. I don't know why—we weren't really doing anything. It's only a massage between friends. Right?

"Is this the place where they're giving out free massages?"

"Omar!" I kick his foot.

But he's not smiling. "Let's get out of here," he says.

"Oh . . . ah, okay," I say, wishing Nicolas would protest.

We drop Nicolas off at the subway on Union Square; then Omar and I walk up to 23rd Street. As we make a left at the Flat Iron Building and cross over toward 8th Avenue, Omar gets creepy. Walk-in-the-park-at-night creepy.

"Do you want Nicolas to be your *caballero*?"

I stop in front of a Home Depot. "Excuse me?"

"Are you planning to be his girlfriend or something?"

"Or something?"

"You know what I mean."

He grabs my hand.

The last time Omar took my hand, we were watching *Harry Potter and the Sorcerer's Stone.* He freaked out over the three-headed dog and squeezed my fingers so tight they practically turned blue. He isn't squeezing them now. He's holding them gently, which freaks me out even more.

"I, uh," I say. I'm very articulate like that.

That's when Omar tries to kiss me. It's real fast and awkward, and I can taste his Dentyne gum all sweet and wintergreen on his breath.

"Whoa!" I pull back.

Omar lets go of my hand and looks around at the other people on the street and the people rushing out of Home Depot as if he's checking what they saw. Then he looks back at me.

"I—"

"Man, that's—"

"I'm—"

"I thought—"

Omar starts slapping himself on the forehead and whispering, "*¡Estúpido!* Stupid! Stupid!"

"Stop that," I say, pulling his hand down before he brains himself.

"I was thinking that since you don't have an escort for your *quince* . . ." Omar rubs his forehead. "I mean, I've known you longer than Nicolas has."

"So?"

"Doesn't seem fair if he's your *caballero*."

"Oh."

I don't say anything else. We keep walking. When we reach our subway stop, I say, "Let's skip the train. Let's ride."

"That's seventy-four blocks."

I shrug. Omar jumps on his board. I jump on mine.

We ride up 8th Avenue. I kick and build momentum and roll past Madison Square Garden on 34th, past the Port Authority Bus Terminal on 42nd. At 48th Street, I fall on the curb next to a Gray Line Sightseeing tour bus. My kneepad slips up, and I bruise myself. I get back up. Omar and I don't make eye contact once.

When we reach 59th Street, I roll over and sit down at the Columbus statue at the center of the traffic circle. I check my knee while Omar stands next to me. He peers down at my knee with a concerned look and then stares up at the Time Warner Building across the traffic circle. This *quinceañera* is making everyone nuts. I wonder if I should just put an end to the whole thing. But the only thought worse than America and my mother arguing over my *quince* and worrying about money is my mother guilt-tripping me for canceling it.

"Are you okay?" Omar finally asks me.

I nod, and we get back on our boards. We roll up to 97th and Central Park West. I'm dripping with sweat and out of breath. We jump off our boards and walk. When we get to my building, Omar stares at the ground.

"Sorry," he mumbles.

Then he walks away without saying good-bye or anything.

I don't know how to fix this. I love Omar and all, just not

that way. How could I? He's . . . well . . . he's Omar. He wears *Incredible Hulk* socks and makes stupid quacking noises during romantic scenes in movies. The socks I could get used to, but no girl wants Daffy Duck as her first real boyfriend. Or her *caballero*. I'm just saying. I don't know what I'm saying. No. I do.

Good times. Yeah. Woo-hoo.

saturday morning

THUMBS

I'm exhausted after addressing only three *quince* envelopes. I drop my pen and tease Natasha out from under my bed, scoop her up, and we both collapse on my comforter. I scratch her ears and under her chin until she purrs. I love that sound. I could listen to it all the time—it's so relaxing. And I know every pet owner thinks this, but Natasha's almost human. No doubt about it. She knows what's going on in this crazy family. Sometimes, when things get really nutty, and TV and skateboarding don't help, she's the only one I can talk to. Her and Fuzzy.

I stop scratching, and Natasha looks at me, annoyed.

"Why'd you stop?" she asks.

"I'm worried," I say.

"Tell me about it," says Natasha. "But keep scratching."

"It's all about this *quince*." I move on to the fur right under her neck, her favorite spot. "Everybody's getting *loco*, worried about money and boys and all kinds of stuff. Now my dress has finally arrived, and mom wants me to keep quiet about it and alter it this week without letting America know— *entre nous*, she says, which is French for lie to your sister— and pick out some heels and choose a *caballero* already and five more *damas* and six more *chambelanes,* so we can start waltzing lessons. And I don't know what America's planning. And these invitations are a pain in the hand, and I still don't know anything about the rent being late, and I'm afraid to ask. Then there's that whole thing about my giving away something from my childhood at the *quince.*"

I look at Fuzzy.

"You wouldn't dare give me away as a symbol of leaving your childhood behind, would you?" Fuzzy is horrified. "You wouldn't dare!"

"It's part of the ritual," I tell him.

"Part of the torture," notes Natasha.

Natasha can be real sarcastic like that. Most Siamese cats are, I've noticed.

"I will not go peacefully," promises Fuzzy. "Don't let my goofy grin fool you. I'm still a bear, you know?"

"No, I won't let them take you. I won't let them. I'll hide you if I have to. I'll—"

"Who are you talking to, *la* woman?"

Stephanie comes into my room, wearing shiny hoop earrings, a slinky charcoal gray dress, and short black boots, holding a stack of her mother's *Essence* magazines and a pint of Ben & Jerry's Phish Food.

Caught. Busted. Flabbergasted (great word). I imagine myself being dragged down Amsterdam Avenue in a straitjacket to the nearest hospital. Talking to a cat *and* a stuffed bear.

But I play it off by immediately launching into a question. "Is Jesse a good kisser?" Jesse has been Stephanie's boyfriend since the end of eighth grade.

"Yes," she answers. "Is Natasha?"

I shake my head at my poor slandered cat. I can tell Natasha is not pleased.

"What about Fuzzy?" Stephanie goes on. "Is he a good kisser?"

Poor Fuzzy. "Never mind," I say and put a pillow over my head.

"I'm just playing." Stephanie sits down on my bed. "Okay, I'm sorry. I'll be mature now."

I take the pillow off my head. "I'm losing it a bit," I admit. "Sometimes I almost get excited to have this Sweet Fifteen, but then all of a sudden I get scared. Really scared. Everything's happening so fast, and . . . I just want to slow it all down."

"Uh-huh."

The truth is, I can talk to Stephanie about things like parties and boys, but not about deposits and loans and rent being late and trying to be Puerto Rican and American at the same time. "Listen, Stephanie, I have to ask you about something. I need you to be serious."

"I am always serious, young lady."

I shoot her a look.

She leans forward, and her braids dangle like tentacles on an octopus. "What?"

"Well, it's about, you know . . . kissing a guy."

"Does this guy have four legs or two?" The seashells in her hair rattle when she laughs.

Natasha shakes her head at me. Even my friends are

clowns! I grab my pillow again.

"Okay, okay!" Stephanie snatches my pillow. "What do you want to know?"

I close my eyes so that I don't have to look at her while I'm confessing. "Well, I just feel like . . . I don't really know what to do."

"Hmm." Stephanie pauses. "What I do is grab hold of the back of his head. Then his tongue can only go in so far."

I open my eyes. "What do you mean?"

"You can make the kiss as short or as deep as you want."

"I see." But I'm not sure I do. "And boys like that?"

"They're in heaven," she assures me. "If you do it right. You know how you can tell whether or not a boy's going to be a bad kisser?"

"How?"

"Check out his thumbs."

"His thumbs?"

"It's a sure sign. Big thumbs, big hands, clumsy hands, clumsy kisser, bad kisser. So, big thumbs . . . don't do it."

She grabs my Fuzzy Bear, checks his thumbs, and starts kissing him. "Oh, Fuzzy, don't stop, don't stop!"

As I watch my best friend violating a stuffed orange bear, I say, real casual, "Omar tried to kiss me yesterday."

"What?!" Stephanie spits out a little orange fur from her bottom lip.

"Yeah. What a jerk, right?"

"Omar?" She puts Fuzzy down. "Your gay best friend, Omar?"

"For the ten-thousandth time, Omar is NOT gay."

"What size are his thumbs?"

"Ack!"

We both laugh, and then we're quiet for a minute. All you can hear is Natasha, purring away.

"Tell me *everything* about you and Omar!"

I hesitate. "You want to see something?"

"What?" she whispers excitedly.

"It's not about Omar. Promise not to tell Erin? She'll just make fun."

"Okay, promise."

I reach under my pillow and show her the Skate15 IM session that I printed out.

She reads it slowly, going over each word.

"So?" I ask. "What do you think?"

"Don't meet with him, whoever he is. He could be a serial killer. You don't want to get serial killed before your fifteenth birthday, do you?"

"I know who it is, silly. It's Nicolas Hernandez."

"Yasmin's cousin?" asks Stephanie. "Did he fall off his skateboard and hit his head?"

"Ha-ha, very funny."

Stephanie studies the IM some more. "He's cute but—"

"I know. He's probably a player."

She holds out the paper. "You want me to destroy this?"

"No!" I snatch it back.

"You really like him, don't you?"

"I don't know."

"Do you think he likes you?"

I gaze at the IM. "Maybe."

Stephanie grabs my face. "Jesus, you're hooked. I can see it in your confused brown eyes. He's got you loony!"

I push her hands away. "I am not loony!"

"That's my *la* woman. The most beautiful, unloony girl I know."

"Yeah, right. It's so funny, huh? It's obvious he finds me irresistible." I cross my eyes and make a face.

Stephanie points at my ponytail. "Must be the scrunchie."

"What if I let Nicolas be my *quince* date? My *caballero*?"

She frowns. "I think we should review my list again, just to be on the safe side."

I groan as she pulls out a laminated card that she carries with her at all times. She hands it to me, but she doesn't have to bother. I can recite Stephanie's "Boyfriend List" by heart (all numbers are of equal importance):

1. Must have at least a B average and be heading for college

2. Must be honest and sincere

3. Must be cute (even if only to you)

4. Must be SINGLE

5. Must be able to form complete sentences

6. Must like going on romantic dates

7. Must like music (especially Beyoncé) and dancing

8. Must have morals

"A *quince* date is not a boyfriend," I protest yet again.

Stephanie shakes her head. "My friend the loon. Who'd've thunk? Since I'm obviously not going to talk you out of this bad boy love, I can only tell you to wait until *after the party* before you let him pounce."

"What is he, a puma?"

"Just go through these magazines and mark which shoes you'd like to wear for your *chinchilla*, okay? And don't you dare tell anybody what happened between me and your bear. If Jesse finds out, he might break up with me. What happens on Sesame Street, stays on Sesame Street. Promise?"

I cross my heart. "I will never tell of your indiscreet moment of passion with my stuffed bear. I promise."

"*Bway-no*," says Stephanie and hands me a magazine. "Shoes. Tell your mom that if you want quality heels, quality costs money."

"Yeah," I say to humor her while I flip through the magazine.

"You want classy not trashy."

"Right."

"And don't worry so much. Your *quesadilla* is going to be great!"

"*Quinceañera*."

"Whatever. Okay?"

"Okay," I say. But it isn't.

Stephanie grabs the remote and switches on the TV for our Saturday morning *My Super Sweet 16* marathon. Part of me wishes I could talk to my friends about *everything*, but Stephanie and I still have a great time watching our trashy TV and pigging out on Ben & Jerry's and talking about guys.

After Stephanie leaves, I take out my stress on my skateboard for the rest of the day. No sign of Omar or Nicolas. I ride around Central Park on my own, low on my board, knees bent, going faster, leaning forward, speeding around the loop till I'm back where I started.

When I get home, I'm so wiped out, I take a nap. I have these really weird dreams. In one, I'm being chased by giant thumbs that keep trying to kiss me. (It's bozo!) I have another dream with Omar in it, except Omar looks a lot like Nicolas. But it's definitely Omar. We're boarding in Riverside Park, and he's totally ignoring me. I try to impress Omar with a jump, but it doesn't work. I tell him, "I don't want things to change!" And then the giant thumbs appear again, on skateboards this time, wearing blue graduation caps and gowns, asking if they can make out with me.

That's when I wake up. America is standing at her closet, holding a dark skirt.

"Good afternoon to you, too." She shakes her head. "If you're stressed out about your green dress arriving this week, don't be. Mami told me about it while we were shopping at the farmer's market this morning. Here's the plan. When she takes you in for the alterations, just stall and say you want to wait until October to make sure the dress fits if you gain a little weight. Then we'll return the dress ourselves and get her deposit back."

"What about the heels?" I ask, still groggy from sleep.

"Tell her you don't see any you like yet. Remember, *our* demands are really for all of us. And by the time I'm through 'negotiating' and getting their deposit money back, I might be able to find it in my heart to go to your anti-*quince* with The Jezebels."

"Yeah?" That perks me up. She is my sister, after all, and it is my birthday party.

"Your job is just to stall," continues America. "I'll take care of the rest."

"Uh, I don't know. . . ." I think about landing the ollie, about Nicolas's hands on my back, about being bold.

I'm afraid, but I say it.

"I want Nicolas Hernandez to be my *caballero*."

America drops her skirt on her bed. She sits down, scowling. "What have you been doing with him?"

"What do you mean? We've just been skating a couple of times."

"Oh, is that what the kids are calling it these days? I've heard that Nicolas gets around, and here you've been practically making music on the old bedsprings with him."

"What bedsprings? I just let him admire my luxurious long brown hair," I tell her.

"Ha! Don't fall for this escort trap. Mami would be more than happy to bring back arranged marriages and get a horse and three pigs from Nicolas in exchange for you."

"I resent that. Everyone knows I'm worth at least two horses and four pigs." But now I feel bad about letting Nicolas change my hair and give me a massage, like I'm turning back time and making things worse for women all over the world. Argh! America took Tomas back, why is what I'm doing so wrong? Why can't everyone leave me alone?

"I know Mami means well," America says, "but it's enough you're having the *quinceañera*. She can't make you have a stupid *caballero*."

"But . . . if I did have a *caballero*, maybe she'd get off both our backs for a bit, don't you think?"

America scowls again.

"Please don't be mad at me, Merry. I'm just thinking about it. It might be fun to have an escort."

"Wow! This is worse than I thought."

America flips open her cell phone.

"Who are you calling?"

She puts up her hand and speaks into her cell. "It's time! Code red!"

Here we go again.

The Jezebels!

saturday night

PETER POOPER

The Jezebels call it "The Mission of *Quinceañera* Future."
We're in Hailey's apartment. Maritza is wearing a bright white
dress, which makes her brown skin look even darker and
prettier, and Hailey stands tall and pale in a green peasant
blouse and long gypsy earrings that swing like crazy every
time she moves. They're guarding me as if I'm expected to
make a run for it and they're ready to take me down.

"Sisters, this meeting is now called to order," announces
America.

"What's this about?" I ask.

"You want to have an escort? You want to become a
woman? It seems you're not convinced yet, little sis."

"Convinced of what?"

"That you'll outgrow the pretty dress, that the heels will
snap, that the diamonds in your tiara are fake cubic zirconias!
Let's go!"

Hailey grabs one of my arms and Maritza the other, and
they drag me toward a room at the end of the long carpeted
hall as I yell, "Help!" and "Where are you taking me?"

"To find the spirit of *caballero* future!" America answers,
and the three of them make scary ghost noises.

"There he is!" shouts Hailey. She points at a blonde, blue-eyed boy in yellow *SpongeBob* pajamas sitting on a little bed, playing a *SpongeBob* video game on the TV. His face is smeared with something that looks like dried chocolate ice cream. "He really likes *SpongeBob*," says Hailey.

"You're going to babysit Hailey's little brother, Peter, tonight," explains America.

"For how much money?" I ask.

America pats me on the shoulder. "Oh, I think the experience will be payment enough."

"It'll help you come to your senses," says Hailey. "See where messing around with boys can lead."

"*Muchacha*," adds Maritza, "after tonight, you'll never think about boys the same way again."

"What about you guys?" I say. "You all have boyfriends."

"Yes, we have boyfriends," agrees America. "But they don't own us. Plus, we're seniors. Old and wise. You are young and need more time to simmer."

"Like a bowl of soup?"

Hailey and Maritza nod as if they understand exactly what America means. If I weren't such a good sister, happy that America's happy with Tomas, I'd tell her that they were the ones who plotted to get them back together.

"Tell you what," says America, "if we come back and you report that you absolutely loved this experience, I will stop fighting with Mami about the *caballero* and we'll drop the 'no escort' rule from your list of demands."

I feel like I'm being asked to choose between having the flu or a parasite, but I nod anyway. "Okay. Ten dollars an hour."

The Jezebels huddle. When they break, America tells me, "Eight dollars an hour, and that's our final offer."

"Deal."

I look at Peter. "What if he gets hungry?"

"Fruit roll-ups," says America.

"What if he wants real food?"

"Hailey?" barks America.

"Mac and cheese in the cabinet next to the sink!" Hailey barks back.

"Mac and cheese in the cabinet next to the sink!" America repeats to me.

"I'm standing right here," I tell them and add, "I'm not changing diapers."

"He's four. He doesn't wear any," Hailey responds.

"Cell inspection!" barks America.

"Cell inspection!" echoes Hailey.

"What're you talking about?" I ask.

"Give us your cell phone," orders Maritza.

I hand America my phone, and she hands it to Hailey, who hands it to Maritza. Maritza takes out her own cell and calls herself with mine. Then she calls Hailey's.

"Okay, all set. You have three ways to reach us." Maritza passes my cell back to Hailey, who passes it to America, who passes it back to me.

"If anything goes wrong, you call us and we'll come right away," says America.

"I have babysitting experience, you know?"

"Who loves you?" asks America. "Who's trying to save you from yourself?"

I shrug. "The Jezebels?"

"Gimme some *azúcar*." America holds out her perfumed cheek. I kiss it and think, if I smelled sweet like America and was blonde like Hailey and looked great in a white dress like Maritza and could walk in heels like my mother, Nicolas would go crazy for me. But I keep that thought to myself.

Then they all kiss me at the same time. I scream as if they were pouring hot lava on me.

"*Nena*," America laughs as I wipe lipstick off my cheeks, "don't show off in front of Hailey and Maritza. You know you love it." She grins.

"Yeah." I roll my eyes. "Where are you guys going, anyway?"

"To a party with Tomas and *Los Guapos*."

"Hey!"

"This lesson is for you, not for us," America argues. "We already know the truth about boys."

"Kiss," says Hailey, and Peter pauses his video game and jumps into her arms and kisses her goodnight and goes back to the game as quickly as he jumped up.

"Good luck trying to get him off that game," Hailey tells me.

"And welcome to *caballero* land," adds America.

Then they're out the door in a cloud of sweet perfume, bright white, and swinging gypsy earrings. I sit on the floor of Peter's room and begin reading *How the García Girls Lost Their Accents* by Julia Alvarez for English class. Before I know it, I feel a tiny finger poking my head. I look up. Peter peers down at me, his face all twisted.

"Bathroom!"

"Okay." I check my watch, noting that only an hour has passed. "Go."

He shakes his head.

"What? You want me to walk you to the bathroom?"

He shakes his head. I sniff the air.

Oh, no!

He starts to cry.

Yup, Hailey's little brother just did a Lenny!

"Why didn't you tell me you had to go earlier?"

He holds up his joystick. "I was playing," he whimpers.

"It's all right. Nothing to be ashamed of. It happened to my sister last week."

He doesn't stop crying. Four-year-olds are a tough crowd.

I think about calling my mother, but she might start interviewing Peter as a candidate for my *caballero*. I think about calling America, but I know that she'll gloat. I'm determined to handle this on my own. Besides, I really could use the money. I want to help out and pay for some of the *quinceañera* myself. All this money that we don't have just to pay for a party. For me. If I could really do it my way—whatever that is—the one thing I know is that it would cost hardly anything. But I could never stop my mom and sister from being involved. That's like trying to stop a hurricane from sinking a dinky little rowboat. And I'm the dinky little rowboat. . . . So the best I can do is throw in my two cents, literally. At the rate I'm going, I'll be able to afford one of the fake jewels on my hideous tiara.

I grab my cell phone and call Stephanie. No answer. Don't panic! I try Erin.

"What's up, dude?" she answers.

"I need your help big-time, dude. America and her Jezebels have left me at Hailey's to babysit her little brother, and he has to go to the bathroom."

"So, duh. Take him to the bathroom."

"Too late."

"What do you mean?" Long pause. "Ewwwww!"

"Help me!"

"What do you want me to do? Call the police? Report a drive-by pooping?"

"Nice one. Help me, please!"

"What have you done for me lately?"

I think for a second. "I'll watch every basketball game with you for three months . . . and I'll listen to you during every inning, no questions asked."

"It's quarter, not inning."

"Whatever!"

"And you'll buy me pizza after every game? Ray's, Famiglia's, Domino's. I'm flexible."

"No."

Slight pause.

"Okay. Deal!" she says. "What do you want me to do?"

"Find Stephanie and both of you come over. ASAP!"

"You got it."

Did I mention I love my friends?

When the two of them arrive twenty minutes later, Erin is wearing a giant backpack and sweats, Stephanie has a red handkerchief on her head to protect her braids, and she's wearing red sweatpants! I haven't seen Stephanie in sweatpants since . . . never.

"What's the backpack for?" I ask.

"Stuff to wash him off with," says Erin.

"No way are we touching him," adds Stephanie.

Erin pulls facemasks, towels, sponges, rubber gloves, Comet, Pine Sol, air freshener, hand sanitizer, and a pair of pliers from her backpack. "You can never be too safe."

Stephanie grabs the pliers.

"Don't be a loon," I say.

"I'll take his top half. You take his legs," Erin orders me.

Great. I get the worst part.

We pull on the rubber gloves and carry Peter to the bathroom and lift him into the tub. He's so confused that he stops crying and just watches our operation. I take off his smelly pajamas and Erin showers him off and Stephanie cleans him up. I dry him and dress him in fresh PJs, and we put him to bed in his *SpongeBob* sheets. He falls asleep as if nothing happened. Oh, to be a little kid again!

We go into the kitchen.

"So what would you have done if neither of us were around?" Stephanie asks.

"She would have pooped her own pants, that's what." Erin laughs.

"I definitely owe you guys."

"So America and The Jezebels set you up, huh?" Erin says. "Those girls are a trip."

"America thinks if I learn how hard it is to raise kids, I'll be cured of ever wanting to mess around with boys."

"Well, I could have told you that, dude."

"Oh yeah." Stephanie snorts. "You're the top authority on boys."

"Hey, I kissed a boy once," insists Erin.

"Uh-huh," says Stephanie. "What's it like?"

"Like chewing on a cow's tongue."

"Ewww!"

"And how do you know what it's like to chew on a cow's tongue?" I ask her.

"Umm, remember that class trip to the children's zoo in seventh? I disappeared for twenty minutes? Ooh, mama!"

"Ewww!"

Erin grabs a pot holder and starts kissing it. "Oh, moo-moo, don't stop, don't stop!"

What is it with my friends making out with inanimate objects?

"I'm such a freakin' lady." Erin grins. "Anyway, I know enough to stay away from boys for now, which is more than I can say for some girls."

She looks at Stephanie.

"The point is not to stay away from them," Stephanie explains. "The point is to be yourself when you're with them."

"That is so wack!" yells Erin. "You sound so *Teen* magazine!"

"Shut up," Stephanie tells her. "Do you want Peter to wake up for round two?"

"Your sister is right, Destiny," Erin goes on. "You don't need anything from boys. You'll just get a Peter Pooper of your own some day, no rush, if that's what you really want.

And you don't really need boys for making babies anymore."

Stephanie shakes her head. "The only reason you think that way is because you don't have a boyfriend like we do. Right, Destiny?"

They both stare at me.

"What? I don't have a boyfriend!"

"What about Mr. Skate15?" demands Stephanie.

"Who is Skate15?" Erin asks.

Stephanie looks at me but when I don't answer, she says, "Nicolas Hernandez. He's going to be her *cuba-lero*."

I don't correct her, but I'm a little pissed that she spilled the beans to Erin after she promised not to.

Erin digs into the fridge and grabs a bottle of ginger ale. "Destiny does NOT like that playa."

"Why do you think he's a player?" I ask, glaring at Stephanie. "What have you heard?"

"I could tell he was a player from the minute I saw you with him on *flan* day." Erin takes a swig straight from the bottle and puts it back in the fridge.

Stephanie takes the ginger ale out of the fridge and hands it back to Erin. "You've bought it. It's yours."

"You still think Nicolas is cute?" I say to Stephanie. She nods. Erin makes gagging noises, but that's all. Thank God.

"Well," I say, "I am thinking he might ask to be my escort to the *quinceañera*."

"NO!!" Stephanie and Erin both shout.

What the heck? Finally, they're in agreement about something and it's about Nicolas *NOT* asking to be my *caballero*?

"You don't wanna get mixed up with a guy like that," warns Erin.

"If he asks you, say no," Stephanie demands.

"A boy like that will kill your brother," Erin sings à la *West Side Story*. "Forget that boy, go get another."

Argh! They're almost as bad as America and my mother.

"Now tell her about Omar trying to kiss you!" says Stephanie.

"What!" yells Erin.

Double argh!

When they leave, I give them both a huge hug, but once they're gone, my head is swimming in confusion. What if Nicolas is a total player? He said he doesn't have a girlfriend, but maybe he's lying, maybe he has *more* than one. If I ask him to be my *caballero*, not only will I seem desperate, I might end up being girlfriend #20,000 and 1.

America and The Jezebels get back from their party a little while later, and I pretend that everything went great.

"Really?" asks Hailey, amazed.

I nod. America and Maritza look at me suspiciously.

Sweet Fifteen.

Yeah, right.

ACT THREE

monday morning

SLUT

Today's breakfast drama: I hear my mom ask my dad, "Did Mr. Fields say anything more about the layoffs?"

"No," he answers. As if that's the end of the story. Mr. Fields is my dad's boss.

"What layoffs?" I ask, entering from stage left.

My father turns to the stove.

My mother grabs cheese, tomatoes, and garlic out of the refrigerator.

"What layoffs?" I ask again.

"Everything's fine, Destiny," my dad assures me as usual.

"We're going to pick up your dress today!" my mom announces. "You come straight home after school. No excuses. And please ask your friends about being your *damas* and *chambelanes*. October is almost here. And you have to finish addressing those invitations. Please, Destiny."

I just nod. My father might be getting laid off, and I'm not supposed to care.

"And," my mother continues, "your *caballero*. You have to choose already, so we can hire a choreographer and start those waltzing rehearsals."

Well, America has let go of the no *caballero* demand. So

now I only have one little problem there: How do I get Nicolas to ask me? But does any of this matter if my father is getting laid off? My parents seem to think it does.

America comes in right on cue. "We're meeting with Tomas about your *quince* music today, Dusty. Gray's Papaya. Six p.m."

ARGHHhhhhhhhhhhhhh!

She asks Mami, "Did you sign Destiny's *quinceañera* demands?"

"I thought we were finished with that *tontería*."

"Just the *caballero* nonsense," replies America. "The other nonsense still stands."

I'm already feeling exhausted, and I still have my first full week of high school ahead of me.

If that's not enough, after washing the breakfast dishes, I grab the garbage and the bag breaks, and coffee grounds and burnt rice and moldy cheese spill out all over the kitchen floor. I want to scream out every curse word I know so loudly that America and my mom will run and hide under the couch all day, like Natasha, and won't come out until the lure of food and water is just too strong.

I never used to feel like this.

I think about tearing down the picture of the Plan B Rodriguez Super Future skateboard from the wall above my bed.

I think about what else I can do to help my parents with money. But nothing comes.

I don't know what else to do, so I leave for school. As I'm waiting for the elevator, the door opens behind me.

"Did you like the *frittata*?"

My dad's in the doorway, dressed for work. Ever since he got hooked on *Top Chef*, he's been making all these new dishes.

"I thought it was an omelet."

"Nope. A *frittata* is prepared in a pan just like an omelet, but then it's broiled."

Who knew? I'm a trusting person. When food is put down in front of me, I eat. I don't ask questions. I don't ask for ID. If it looks like food, I take its word for it. Broiled or not.

"Hey, Papi? I was thinking . . . Maybe I could help out and pay for some of the *quinceañera* myself?"

"That's not necessary," he says. "You want a summer job, that's fine. During school, you concentrate on school."

"I could give skateboarding lessons," I suggest. "To little kids in the building."

I just came up with that one.

My father shakes his head. "Only one more month of baseball left, worry about that."

He smiles at me, but he seems tired. I smile back. We're quiet until the elevator arrives.

"Floor?" my father asks.

"Lobby, please, Mr. Lozada."

"Your wish is my command."

He presses the L button.

The elevator stalls, a normal occurrence in our building.

"C'mon, c'mon. Not today!" My father pushes the L button really hard.

"Dad?"

He pushes the button again and again.

"Maybe we should press the emergency button?" I ask.

"This isn't an emergency. It's just this old elevator."

"Can we afford this *quinceañera*?" I ask suddenly, even though I know the answer. I just want someone to tell me the truth and stop trying to protect me. "Are you being laid off from work?"

He keeps pushing the button.

"Papi, please. I'm going to be fifteen soon. You can tell me what's going on."

He hesitates. "Well," he says finally, "there have been some layoffs at my job. And the rent just went up. The car keeps breaking down so we might need a new one, and we're just trying to catch up with the bills, but they're piling faster than the money is coming in right now. . . ." He stops and takes a deep breath and looks me in the eye. "But we have everything under control. You don't need to worry."

The elevator begins moving again.

The more my dad tells me not to worry, the more worried I am. But what can I do when no one will let me do anything?

Worry!

We're walking to school, and I'm lost in my thoughts when Stephanie whispers, "Did you hear?"

"What?"

"There's a rumor going around that Yasmin Hernandez is already *la* woman."

"What does *that* mean?" asks Erin.

"Well, I heard from Ryan that Yasmin's a slut and had sex

with a bunch of boys in Central Park," says Stephanie.

OMG! Yasmin's a Jezebel. Only the real thing.

"Ryan's not one to talk," I say. "If you're a girl with a pulse, Ryan will make out with you."

Erin laughs and slaps me on the back too hard.

"How does Ryan know, anyway?" I ask.

"Amanda told him."

"Amanda's probably just mad at Yasmin about something," I declare as we keep walking. "Amanda kisses Yasmin's butt one minute, getting her to trust her and tell her stuff, and then I'm sure she goes and uses it all against her."

"I don't know," says Stephanie. "There's also a rumor that Yasmin is having sex with teachers."

"Mr. Porton?" Erin laughs. "Wow!"

Geeky Yasmin, who used to always follow me and my friends around, with those magnifying lens glasses and that annoying laugh. Is this really the new you?

"I mean, even if rumors aren't one hundred percent true," Stephanie goes on, "there's usually some kernel, right?"

Erin nods. "I think there must be some reason they catch on."

"Nicolas Hernandez is going to be my *caballero*," I announce, to change the subject.

"Are you sure?" asks Stephanie, as we cross the street.

"Has Mr. Smoothie asked you?" asks Erin.

"Not yet," I admit. "But babysitting went so well, with a little help from my friends, that America now accepts I can handle any boy that comes my way."

"I heard the same thing about Yasmin!" jokes Erin.

"That's cold." Stephanie shakes the seashells in her hair.

Hold the curtain! Outside school, Amanda and Melanie walk by, sizing me up and down from my scrunchie-loving head to my Converse sneakers. They're playing their favorite game where they say stuff to the new nerdy kids like, "Don't I know you from someplace, fatty?" and "Hey, ugly, what're you lookin' at?" Then they laugh hysterically.

"Why did Yasmin ever want to be friends with them?" says Stephanie as we go inside.

"I think maybe I was like that sometimes with The Jezebels," I tell her. "Hanging around, hoping to be included, thinking they're absolutely the coolest. I guess I still am. Like maybe if I hang out with them, I'll finally find the answer."

"What answer?" asks Erin.

"THE SECRET TO BEING COOL."

"Just ask me," says Erin.

"She said cool not ghoul." Stephanie laughs as we stroll past the reception desk.

"Maybe that's how Yasmin feels," I add. "Like Amanda might know the secret."

"Why are you defending Yasmin so much?" asks Stephanie.

"Don't you know? Yasmin is her new cousin-in-law," says Erin.

"Ha-ha. Maybe something happened to Yasmin that summer after seventh, something that made her turn herself into this whole other person."

We reach the theater, where I've got drama class first period this morning. Stephanie and Erin stop with me.

"Whatever made it happen," warns Stephanie, "Yasmin is now the Official School Slut."

"I hear the job comes with its own office and keys to all the supply closets," Erin jokes again.

"That's not funny," I say.

"No, it's not," agrees Stephanie with a little smile. "Poor girl's named after a birth control pill. It's really not her fault."

"You're being mean," I tell them.

It's one thing for Yasmin to transform into a hottie, but it's another for everyone to start calling her a slut. Not exactly a great way to start off high school. Getting a rep like that can stay with you for a long time.

"We're just joking." Stephanie gives me a little bump with her hip. "But you're right. Let's stop."

I watch them head off for their classes, and then I go into drama. I thought I was the first one, but I hear a book bag being unzipped.

Yasmin! Sitting in the back of the theater!

I pray she didn't hear us.

I nod at her, and she nods, too. I sit in front of her.

"You were really good in your monologue last week," I tell her, mostly because it's true but also because I feel guilty that we were talking crap about her.

"Was I? You, too," she says.

"No. I totally sucked. I could hardly pronounce anything."

She pulls her monologue out of her bag. I see that it's all marked up with notes. She really took it seriously. "Hey! After school today, do you want to hang out in the park with me and some guys from my art class?" she asks.

"Uh . . ." Is she inviting me to be her Official Co-Slut or something? I don't want to believe the rumors, but in some ways, it doesn't even matter. The last Official School Slut had to switch schools because kids made fun of her every day. And she wasn't even sexy like Yasmin is now. She had greasy black hair and wore wool dresses and funny shoes. But supposedly she did something with a gang of boys in the school basement.

"I don't think I can," I tell her. "I have to study for a history quiz." It's a total lie. I cross my fingers that Yasmin doesn't know Mr. Diamant never gives quizzes. Why did I even lie? I remember I'm supposed to do *quince* stuff after school.

Yasmin shoots me a funny look, like she's going to cry. "Okay. I was just asking." Then she adds, almost to herself, "Do you ever think that if you never saw most of the people you know again, it wouldn't bother you?"

Whoa! It's such a heavy thing to say that I worry a little about Yasmin's mental health. But I know she's talking about Amanda and Melanie.

We sit there for what feels like forever. Then we stare off in opposite directions, reading over our monologues, and we . . . don't . . . say . . . a . . . single . . . word . . . to each other.

I skipped the caf on Friday last week and ate alone at a falafel spot, because at school they were serving those yummy gray, boiled hot dogs, but today I skip the caf so that I'm not seen with Yasmin, who would probably try and sit with me again. In high school, you're allowed to leave during lunch as long as you go somewhere nearby, so I just drink a Coke at McDonald's by myself. I'll probably have to eat lunch out on my own until this slut thing blows over or until Yasmin switches schools, whichever comes first. I feel like a turd.

After school, Omar walks past me on the street as if I'm invisible. He's wearing a brand-new *Iron Man* T-shirt and jeans, drinking a Yoo-hoo and shoveling one of those little McDonald's apple pies into his mouth. I haven't seen or heard from him all weekend. No text, no call, no e-mail. That never happens. I run and catch up to him.

"Hey!"

He stops chewing, but he's all quiet and ashamed looking. Omar is still embarrassed about the kiss thing!

I decide all is forgiven. No hard feelings. I poke him in the ribs to let him know, but he doesn't laugh. Omar always laughs when I poke him in the ribs. It's like his Prozac.

Nothing. Silence.

He starts to walk away, but I pull him back. He tries again, but I pull him back even harder.

"Man," he says, "you're stronger than you look."

"C'mon. Let's go get our boards and head to the park."

We walk, side by side, and things almost feel like they're back to normal. Then Omar gets this gleam in his eyes and leans in toward my face. He can't be serious! But instead of kissing me, he burps really loudly.

I'm chasing him north along Columbus Avenue when I hear the familiar cry of "Destiny!"

It's my red balloon: my mother's across the street in the Pontiac, motor running, waving a bag of Dunkin' Donuts. Of course, Omar runs toward the car, grabs the donuts, and jumps in. When I cross over, my mom asks me, "Well? Ready to get your dress altered?"

"That's today?" How did I forget again? Wishful thinking? Denial?

"Did you get the rest of your *damas* and *chambelanes* and finish addressing your invitations?"

"Uh, not since this morning."

"*Ay*, Destiny!"

I squeeze into the front seat. Behind me, Omar's munching on a Boston Cream like it might be snatched away any minute. He doesn't even mind that we're going to a dress shop.

We drive across Central Park to Lexington Avenue, then head north till we reach La Bridal. My mom finds a parking spot right in front, and we get out. A Latino couple is kissing by the window display.

In the shop, romantic elevator music plays. I try on my dress and a pair of matching heels.

Omar nods at my long, deep dark emerald green—and amazingly, not completely hideous—dress and my mother claps. I try to walk in the heels and nearly break my neck.

"It's okay," I say, regaining my balance and looking at myself in the mirror. "But the dress is too long and too pouffy."

My mom starts tugging at the dress. "Maybe it is a little roomy. We can have it taken in a little here . . . and here . . ."

I smile and curtsey at Omar as she keeps tugging.

Then I remember what America said: stall and maybe we can return the dress and the heels and get the deposit back.

"You know, Mami, I might gain weight between now and my birthday."

That seems to make her stop and think, so I keep going.

"Why don't we wait until the beginning of October? That would still give us almost a month to have the dress taken in a little, if we need to."

My mom's unsure.

"I really like this dress, and I want to make sure it fits, and why get the shoes until we have the dress?"

It's not a complete lie, and it seems to convince her. She kisses me on the cheek.

"We'll wait until October first. In the meantime . . ."

She launches herself at some fake diamond tiaras at the other end of the store.

Omar points at me. "I like it."

"What?"

He points at the dress. "I said, I like it."

"Why?"

"It's a pretty color."

I look at him, skeptical. "I feel stupid."

"You do? Why?"

"I don't know. I just feel funny. None of this feels right."

Omar scans the store. His eyes stop on a tuxedo.

"It's kind of strange you and Nicolas are friends," I say.

"Why is it strange?" Omar asks defensively.

I mean it's strange because Nicolas has this mysterious tough-guy thing going, and that's so not Omar. The last tough-guy thing Omar did was almost killing himself after dousing his *chimichanga* with Crazy Jerry's Brain Damage Hot Sauce. But I can tell by Omar's face that he thinks I mean it's strange because Nicolas is such a cool guy: why would he hang with someone like Omar? Okay, it's true, Omar's a nerd and a brainiac. He does really well in school and likes to read comic books, and he watches cartoons like it's a religion, dresses like Spider-Man every Halloween, and plays Guitar Hero like it's a part-time job. I peek at his thumbs, which are kind of small. According to Stephanie's theory, if you believe it, he's a good kisser. Omar. Ha!

I wish Omar wasn't so insecure. He's really smart and funny, and he's got all this potential. He just doesn't know it yet.

"No, I mean—" Omar waits for me to finish. It's no use. Something has changed between us. I should just stop talking.

So I do.

I look at the price tag on my dress: $595.00.

Jeez!

monday at 6:30 p.m.

TOMAS AND BALA

I'm leaning against the window of Gray's Papaya on 72nd and Amsterdam, the local spot for cheap hot dogs and papaya juice. America, The Jezebels, and I are meeting Tomas and then heading over to his apartment on West 46th and 10th Avenue. His neighborhood was named Hell's Kitchen on account of it once being full of dirty tenements and factories and so dangerous that even cops were afraid to go there. It's pretty safe and clean and expensive now, and some people tried calling it "Clinton," but we don't. We're going there to listen to the songs that Tomas has written for my *quince.*

But Tomas is late. My sister checks her watch again. Hailey, who is a vegetarian, refuses to lean against the "infected" Gray's Papaya window and stands near the curb.

I don't really mind that Tomas isn't here yet because I don't feel like dealing with the *quince* madness. But America's not too happy about it. She goes to the corner to look for him.

"So how are you doing?" Maritza asks.

"Good," I lie.

"You have everything you want, right? Tomas and America are back together. You can have some cute boy for your *caballero*. Everybody's going to be happy. You'll see. Aren't you happy?"

"I guess."

America comes back with a terrible scowl on her face, and now we all go searching for Tomas and find him outside McDonald's on 71st and Broadway, with this pretty Indian girl. He's wearing tight jeans over his lanky legs, his rock star sunglasses resting on the tip of his nose.

As we get closer, I notice that his eyes are red and he smells like smoke. America's growling, she's so angry. The girl Tomas is talking to has long-long-long black hair and her nose pierced, and she's wearing a T-shirt that says "KARMA IS A BEACH." She's talking loudly to Tomas about some band I've never heard of, and he's totally not noticing America, so she charges over and yells, "Tomas, we've been waiting for half an hour! What the hell are you doing?"

Tomas turns to the Indian girl. "Hey, this is my girlfriend, America. America, this is Bala. She goes to my school. Bala's a drummer."

Tomas and *Los Guapos* go to Music and Art High School behind Lincoln Center. It's the school where kids with amazing incredible talent go. Bala looks at America. It's not a nice look. "I didn't know you had a girlfriend," she says.

"We're supposed to go over the music," America plows on. "Talk about the *quinceañera*!"

Bala shrugs. "It's all right, Tomas. You guys talk. I have that show at school to get ready for anyway. Text me later."

America shoots her a deadly scowl. Bala just smiles and adds, "You should come see me play tonight, Tomas. It's gonna be a real scene."

"Can we start, *now*, Tomas?" America demands. "Destiny has homework to do, and you've already wasted enough of her time."

Tomas kisses Bala quickly on the cheek, and she grins at him and says, "peace out" before she walks off. As soon as she's gone, America turns to Tomas with her hands on her hips. Maritza and Hailey have their arms crossed, and they're shaking their heads. They all look like they want to tear him from hot dog to bun. I stand back so I won't get hit in the eye with any flying body parts. (A spleen in the eye really hurts. Or so I've heard.)

"Where were you?" asks America.

"Whaddaya mean? I was with Bala. She's in my music class."

"No, I mean last night," America says. "Were you with Bala then, too?"

"Don't be crazy. I told you, I was at Kyle's until ten playing video games."

"Oh, that's funny," says Hailey. "Kyle was with me last night until ten."

"I mean Byron's," Tomas says quickly.

Maritza shakes her head. "I was with Byron until eleven."

Hailey stares at Tomas. "We defended you."

Tomas turns to America. "Baby—"

America huffs and puffs and tries to leave, but Tomas grabs her and tries to kiss her passionately like she's asthmatic and he's an air pump. Outside McDonald's!!! America just pushes him away.

"Is that how you do it with Bala?" asks Hailey.

"You're disgusting." Maritza has tears in her eyes like he's *her* cheating boyfriend.

"Jesus! I give up! I'm tired of your jealousy, America," Tomas says.

"It's not jealousy," America snarls. "It's all true."

"What did I do?" he asks. They all give him a disgusted look, and he yells, "That was last year!"

They turn their backs on him, arms crossed.

Oh, brother. Stay tuned for the next episode of *As the Quince Turns.*

"Are we going to look at the new songs?" I ask in my most calm and mature voice.

"No," says America. "I changed my mind. Let's go home, girls."

"Fine," says Tomas. "Leave!"

So we do.

At the corner, America stops and nods at Hailey and Maritza. "Follow him."

Hailey and Maritza nod back and take off. I'm afraid this means America has gone back to the obsessive zone. Welcome to Stalker High.

When America and I get home, she raids the refrigerator and the cupboards, stocking up on Double Stuffed Oreos and leftovers of my dad's famous mac and cheese, grabbing a Fresca and opening it too quickly so that the foam erupts and slides down the bottle like a volcano.

My mother comes in. "What happened?"

"I don't feel well." America groans.

"Sit down," coos my mother and gives me a look. I shrug.

My sister sits, and my mom helps her out of her combat boots and feels her forehead. America puts her arms around my mother's waist and leans on her stomach.

Mami guides America to our bedroom and helps her get into bed, then goes back to the kitchen to reheat the mac and cheese. I peek into the room. America rolls over to face the wall and throws her comforter over her head. I go to the computer and quietly do my homework. After a while, The Jezebels come in.

"Tomas will NOT be playing at your *quinceañera*!" Maritza announces.

"What did you see?" asks America, pulling the comforter off her head.

"We caught him with that drummer, Bala! He tried to pretend like nothing was happening, but we saw them kissing outside Music and Art."

"Pig!" America shouts.

"Who? Him or Bala?" I ask, swiveling around on the computer chair.

"Both!" says Hailey.

Maritza nods at Hailey. "You have to tell her."

Hailey shakes her head. "*You* tell her."

"Tell me what?" America sits up in bed.

For some reason, they all look at me.

"Well, um, your Jezebels may have been plotting to get you and Tomas back together," I say. "It may have been their idea that *Los Guapos* call Mami and offer to play at my *quince*."

America glares at me.

"Wasn't my idea," I say.

"Wow." America stares at Hailey and Maritza. "I think it's pretty hypocritical, a feminist group wanting me to get past cheating."

"We didn't want you to get past cheating," Hailey says, lingering by the door where it's safe.

Maritza sits on America's bed. "We wanted you to forgive someone we thought had made a mistake or at least had the potential to change."

"We were wrong about him," Hailey admits, "but if he really had changed and you still loved him . . ."

"You thought he'd changed, too, didn't you?" asks Maritza and taps America's knee.

"You guys kept bringing him up, and he seemed so sincere. What was I supposed to think?"

"C'mon." Hailey steps away from the door. "Admit it was better when we were all together, Maritza and Byron, me and Kyle, you and Tomas. After you guys broke up—"

"Because he CHEATED ON ME," America interrupts.

"You know, there was all this serious tension, negative energy," Hailey finishes.

Maritza nods. "We all stopped hanging out together, doing the fun stuff we used to do."

"You expected me to hang out with my ex just so things could feel the way they used to?"

"Of course not," says Maritza. "It was just really uncomfortable. I mean, we were pissed at Tomas, too, and that made things weird with Byron and Kyle."

America scowls at Hailey and Maritza. "It would have

been nice if we women had stuck together."

"America," Hailey snaps, "we did stick with you. We just want you to be happy."

Silence. It seems like everybody is trying to make everybody happy, and nobody is.

America sighs. "Look, guys, I know you didn't mean me any harm. I accept your selfishness as just a natural need to feel comfortable, to keep things from changing. And I'm the one who took Tomas back, so I guess I felt that need, too. But the fact is, things change."

We all nod in agreement, which feels good considering that things had gotten a teeny bit tense.

"It's our last year in high school, The Jezebels and *Los Guapos*, and I wanted us all to be together, too," says America. "But I knew deep down that it wasn't going to work."

"How did you know?" asks Maritza.

"I just had a feeling. I know Tomas. I could tell. But I wanted to be wrong."

"Well," says Hailey, "you were right." She sits by Maritza at the end of America's bed.

"Haven't you figured this out about my sister?" I ask. "She is never, ever wrong. How does it feel to always be right?" I ask America.

"It's exhausting," she complains.

I wonder if part of America is really just as surprised and disappointed in Tomas as we are, but she can't admit it. If this helps her feel better, though, it works for me.

Except now we'll have to pay for a band, which will be another expense. Somebody call Bellevue. I'm ready.

"Sleepover!" yells Maritza.

"We have school tomorrow," grumbles America.

"We can do our homework together," says Hailey. "We'll do homework, eat junk, play some Ms. Pac Man, talk about boys—"

We all shoot Hailey a look. Hailey corrects herself. "No, forget boys! We have a lot of other things to talk about."

"Do you see what I'm talking about now, Dusty?" America clicks on the TV and presses play on a saved *My Super Sweet 16* episode. "Look at that. You want to be like those brain-dead, spoiled, self-centered rich girls whose *only* concern is shopping and boys?"

"No," I tell her.

America points at the TV. "So why do you watch this junk? I saw one episode where some girl actually rented hot male escorts for her party like they were prostitutes."

"They're not?" jokes Maritza. "I have to make a phone call."

"One girl," America continues, ignoring her, "had her boyfriend compete with a cuter guy to see who would be her escort. Her boyfriend won, and she still picked the cuter one."

"I saw that one!" exclaims Hailey. "Her boyfriend had no backbone at all! Humiliating!"

"So what were you doing watching my show?" I ask America.

America blushes and flips the channel to PBS. "Well, I have to know what the enemy is thinking."

"It wasn't because the show is stupid junky fun?" asks Hailey.

"I don't do stupid junky fun," says America and jumps out of bed. "I'm a senior. C'mon Jezebels, let's go drown our sorrows in mac 'n' cheese."

They head for the kitchen, and I get back on the computer.

I'm checking my e-mail when Nicolas pops up again:

    Skate15: wassup, sweetie!

    (Sweetie?)

    DLo: Where have u been? U IM me and then ur just gone. Not fair.

    Skate15: i'm with you now, beautiful.

    DLo: Under my bed?

    Skate15: (cough, cough, cough) exactly.

We start IMing back and forth, and before you know it . . .

    DLo: Oh my god! I'm late for dinner.

    Skate15: me 2. i didn't even notice. so . . . we should meet up.

    DLo: I thought you'd never ask!!!

    Skate15: lincoln center fountain? tomorrow @ 4?

    DLo: Ok.

    Skate15: goodnight . . . starz.

    DLo: Starz?

    Skate15: ur eyes r like 2 twinkling starz.

Before I can respond, he signs off. Two twinkling starz? Kind of corny? But also kind of sweet. I didn't know Nicolas had it in him. He must *really* like me. I know what happened with Tomas. I know all that supposed player stuff about Nicolas. But I also know he's different with me. I'm different. We're different together. I can feel it. He's going to ask me. I knew it! How crazy is that?

    My Skate15.

    My *caballero.*

tuesday

SKATE15

The next morning I enter the kitchen humming. I'm so freaking happy!

It's *destiny*.

In the dictionary, destiny is "a predetermined course of events," which basically means that whatever happens to you has already been planned. My mother always tells us that if something is meant to be, it'll be. My sister insists that's crap; if you sit around waiting for stuff to happen, it won't. But maybe my *quince* and Nicolas were both meant to be.

"Morning, Papi! Morning, Mami!"

"Hi, honey." My father is making *huevos rancheros*. I kiss his cheek.

My mom is sitting at the kitchen table with her blue coffee mug, pink folder, and a yellow pad. She hands me the rest of my unaddressed *quince* invitations. "We're going over to Julia's for dinner tomorrow night," she tells me.

"Why?" I ask. Julia is Mrs. Hernandez.

"We haven't been there in a long time," my father says, taking some *tortillas* out of the fridge. He doesn't want me to know that they're borrowing money from Mrs. Hernandez, but I do. America told me. I wonder if Yasmin knows, too?

My parents *never* borrow money; they're only doing it for my *quinceañera*. But I don't feel guilty this time because I also know that everything is going to work out. *Destiny.*

"I made your trial appointment for hair, makeup, and nails," my mother announces, reading from her yellow pad. "I need you to start preparing a speech to thank your family and guests. I'm talking to a friend of your father's about the new band." She pauses, raising a dyed blonde eyebrow. "So is Nicolas Hernandez your *caballero*?"

My father turns, holding a can of black beans.

My mouth drops open. Sometimes she's a lot like America—she knows everything.

"Um . . ." I say.

"Good!" My mother claps her hands. "Now get me those *damas* and *chambelanes* this week, and we can finally hire a choreographer for dance lessons. A little over a month is not great but—"

I run at my mother and sit on her lap. It works. She changes the subject.

"How did you sleep, heavy one?" My mother groans.

"I slept great. How about you guys?"

"Never better," my father answers, and I almost believe him.

"How's school?" asks my mother.

"Yesterday, Mr. Diamant said I was the most astute history student he's ever had!"

"Of course you're astute," agrees my father, chopping onions and tomatoes. "Your mother's astute. Your grandmother was astute. You come from a long line of 'stutes.'"

I laugh. Maybe a little too loud, because both my parents stare at me like they're searching for the cuckoo's nest I just flew over.

"Destiny? Are you okay, *hija*?" my mom asks.

"Yeah. Why?"

"You come in here, humming, kissing, laughing, sitting on your mother's lap," says my dad. "Did you hit the *número* or something?"

"No lottery, I'm just happy." I jump up to get some silverware. "I love my life, that's all. Don't you ever wake up feeling like that?"

My dad thinks a moment. "Nope." I don't believe him.

"Shut up, Jon. You'll be happy and you'll like it." My mom goes over and kisses his cheek and slaps his butt. "Get back to work!"

"*Sí, señora.*"

I love my parents! I love America. I love my friends. I love my high school. I love my apartment building. I love Central Park. I love September. I even love my *quinceañera*.

The day passes by faster than a soccer ball at the World Cup. Nothing gets me down, not the B- I get on my geometry test. Not even the idea of dinner at Yasmin's tomorrow.

After school, I go home and shower and change into a baby blue skirt and a paisley top that I keep all the way in the back of my closet, for emergency use only. I spray myself with some of America's perfume and put a rose from my mother's kitchen vase in my hair, which I wear down. Then I head over to Lincoln Center, where they have all this cultural stuff like plays, operas, classical music, jazz, and ballet, and I'm sitting at the fountain waiting for Nicolas to show up when . . .

Omar rides by on his skateboard.

Damn!

I try to hide my face, but he skates over.

"It's a little early for Halloween." He kicks his board up into his hands.

I pull the flower out of my hair. "Gee, thanks."

"No . . . I mean . . . what're you doing?"

"Nothing. Meeting Stephanie. Going shopping."

"For what?" he asks and plays with the wheels on his board.

I blink. "I don't know."

"You don't know?"

I glance at the white stone walls of the New York City Opera and think of Italy. "Cheese."

"Cheese?"

I glance back at Omar. "My father wants some special cheeses for my *quinceañera*. Stephanie is helping me scout our options."

"Well, you could get blue cheese. Did you know that Gorgonzola is one of the oldest kinds of blue cheese, going back to about 800 AD or something like that?" Omar smiles like a dope and touches the sleeve of my blouse. "You always dress up like this for Gorgonzola?"

"I'm not dressed up." I slap his hand away.

"Sure. Okay."

He sits down next to me, and I want to knock him into the fountain.

"What're you doing?" I ask him.

"I'll wait with you." He starts swinging his skinny legs.

"No! You can't wait with me!" I stand up.

"Why not?"

"Because . . . Stephanie is a very private person."

"Stephanie? Private? About cheese?"

"She's been bummed out lately."

"Why?" Omar stands, too.

"She just found out . . . she has an allergy." (Yes, I suck at thinking fast.) "You really need to go."

"An allergy?"

"C'mon, Omar, before she gets here."

"Okay, okay." Omar gets back on his skateboard, rolls a bit, then stops. "Can I ask you something? It's really important."

I sit back down and sigh a deep sigh worthy of my mother or America. "What?"

"Can I call you starz?"

He smiles that dopey smile, waiting for me to react.

It slowly sinks in.

I cannot BELIEVE it!

Omar

is

Skate15!

Omar laughs. "I used my mom's cell to text you!"

I'm so furious that I can't even look at him. I just stand up and walk away without a word while Omar yells, "Destiny! Destiny! C'mon!" But I keep walking.

And I know.

I know like I know my own name. Like I know A-Rod is a baseball player, not a bar for hanging curtains. Like I know smoking causes cancer. Like I know suspenders don't go with shorts (unless you're Stephanie). Like I know this *quince* is ruining my life.

I know that I will never-ever-never-ever talk to Omar again.

wednesday night

THE HORROR

Forget what I said about dinner with Yasmin and her family not getting me down. That was when I thought Nicolas was maybe in love with me. Now that I know he's not, the thought of it is torture.

"Wow!" exclaims America, watching me slam drawers on ugly skirts and yank stupid blouses from their hangers. "You really don't want to go to Mr. and Mrs. H's tonight, huh?"

I throw myself on my bed. "It's not just that."

I pause, not sure if I want to tell America about Omar or not. It's just so mortifying.

"What?"

I look at my sister, and it hits me that next year, she won't be here for me to talk to.

"It's Omar," I tell her.

"What did he do now?" she asks.

"I've been IMing with Nicolas."

"You've been IMing with Nicolas Hernandez?"

"Yeah, but it wasn't Nicolas Hernandez."

"You've been IMing with Nicolas Hernandez, but it wasn't Nicolas Hernandez?"

"I *thought* it was Nicolas Hernandez. We had these great, sweet conversations on IM and totally connected—"

"You connected with Nicolas?"

"Yeah, but it wasn't him. It was Skate15."

"Who the heck is Skate15?" America asks.

"Nicolas!"

"That's what I said."

"But it wasn't Nicolas," I say.

"It was Skate15?" she asks, starting to get it.

"Right."

"Skate15 who was Nicolas but wasn't?"

"Exactly."

"Of course."

"So I finally went out to meet Skate15," I say. "Skate15, who I thought was Nicolas, but he turned out to be—"

"Omar!" yells America, clapping her hands together.

"Exactly!"

"So Omar was talking all sweet to you on IM?"

"Yeah."

"Aw. That's kind of cute, if you think about it."

"I don't think it's cute," I snap.

What would be cute is if Nicolas was Skate15 and we were officially boyfriend and girlfriend and he'd be the one to escort me to my stupid *quinceañera,* which we can't afford, so we now have to go over to the Hernandezes and get a loan. What would also be cute is if the Hernandezes were my *padrinos,* my godparents, because according to *quinceañera* law, the money could be a gift, and not a loan.

"Let's just get this dinner over with." I sigh.

Everyone gets dressed in their best clothes and piles into the Pontiac. When it starts heading east, I consider throwing myself from the car. A few broken bones should do it.

We cross Central Park and arrive at the Hernandezes' building on East 86th Street. I'm so embarrassed that we're here to borrow money, not only in front of Yasmin but also in front of Nicolas, who is *not* in love with me. Maybe we can still stop this somehow.

But before I can think of a way, we're in Yasmin's fancy lobby and a doorman is buzzing their apartment.

We're allowed up and greeted at the apartment door by Mr. Hernandez. He's a short, bald man with droopy eyes, wearing gray slacks, a white dress shirt, and a straw fedora hat with a red band.

"*¡Familia!*" Mrs. Hernandez waves the fat diamond ring on her hand as she speaks. I'd really hate to be like Mrs. H. She tries to act like she's not growing old. At Yasmin's *quince*, she wore this tight cream-colored silk dress that made her look like a giant burrito, with refried beans hanging out of the sides, and she kept giggling with all of Yasmin's friends, especially the boys. How can someone so rich have such a huge complex and be so ridiculous? I wish Mrs. H would just act natural, but America says she's really unhappy and unsatisfied with her life; she's so brainwashed with all this status stuff, she doesn't have time to be herself.

Mrs. H gives us a short tour to show how she's remodeled the apartment. The living room is filled with fancy chairs, couches, mirrors, lamps, and rugs that look like something Marie Antoinette would pick out. A white marble coffee table, fake flowers, and a leather armchair face a ginormous 4 million-inch flat-screen TV. I've seen smaller movie screens.

The place is so neat and spotless it's like no one lives here.

We go to Yasmin's bedroom next. I vaguely remember her old room from a birthday party when we were kids, before they moved to this place, when they didn't use to be so rich. It was super small and cluttered, and her bedroom was really part of the living room that had been sectioned off with a flowered curtain. America and I have always had to share a room, but at least it has a door.

Yasmin's new bedroom is huge. She has a king-size bed, and her dressers are white and pink. Everything matches, like in a magazine. Mrs. H. tells us that Nicolas is sleeping on the pull-out couch in the living room for now, but they're hiring a contractor to split Yasmin's room into two bedrooms. I guess it's nice of the Hernandezes to do that for Nicolas. It must mean he'll be staying here for a while?

I spot Yasmin and Nicolas sitting at the long table in the dining room. Yasmin seems pissed. She's wearing a tight blouse and short white skirt and, from where I'm standing, I can almost tell what color underwear she chose this morning. Nicolas is two chairs to her right, with his back to her. It looks like maybe they've had a fight. She's shaking her head and he's jiggling his knee up and down, and they're both scowling off in opposite directions. My mother and Mrs. H ramble on a bit about the old days and how in Isabela the kids were never like these "out-of-control New York kids." We finally sit for dinner before they start singing the Puerto Rican national anthem.

During dinner, Yasmin doesn't talk. Nicolas smiles and kicks my foot under the table once or twice. But he's not kicking my foot because he's my Skate15; he's kicking my foot because he thinks it's cute. Nothing feels very cute right now.

America talks about feminism and the *quince* and why she's still not going.

Mrs. H frowns and keeps repeating, "The ideas these girls have. It's not good."

"Well," says my dad gently, "I think it's healthy. Doubt gives you an education."

"As long as they stick to practical stuff," says Mr. H with his mouth full of *arroz con pollo.*

Yasmin rolls her eyes.

To my amazement, my dad nods weakly. I'll bet he feels like he has to agree because of the loan.

But my mom defends America, saying, "She's young, and young people have to exercise their brains with new ideas." America almost faints (or pretends to, anyway).

Mrs. H turns to me. "So, how is the *quince* coming along?"

"I just made Destiny trial appointments for hair, makeup, and nails," answers my mother. "She's writing a speech to thank family and guests, and I'm talking to *Don* Rosario about the music. Oh, and we're sending the invitations out this weekend. No excuses. *Sí*, Destiny?"

I nod. "*Sí.*"

"How is the dress?" Mrs. H asks me.

"Destiny wants to wait to alter the dress in October," my mother answers for me again. "She's afraid she'll gain weight."

"But she's so skinny!" Mr. H laughs.

"It's a good idea," says Mrs. H. "What about the *caballero*?"

Nicolas and Yasmin both look at me.

"Work in progress," my mother answers and smiles at Nicolas. He smiles back. Then he kicks my foot again, but it's not really a kick, more of a tap, and even though he's not my Skate15, maybe he does like me that way after all? The next time he taps my foot, I tap his and he taps mine and we just keep tapping, grinning at each other. Out of the corner of my eye, I watch Yasmin peer under the table and frown. Why is she being such a downer? I swear, if Nicolas wasn't her cousin, I'd say she was jealous!

"Actually, Destiny's not wearing a dress or heels," America announces, divulging *our* secret plan. "We're probably getting a refund or maybe she can save the dress for her graduation where she can stand up alone and proud."

"America!" snaps my father. "Not now."

Mrs. H glances at Yasmin and slaps my mother's arm. "Kids!" She laughs with her mouth open so wide I can see all her gold fillings.

Mr. H mutters something to Nicolas about dessert, adjusting his hat.

"Who wants some bread pudding?" asks Mrs. H.

Great. I HATE bread pudding.

At last, the meal of torture is over (well, not all torture, thanks to some foot tapping). Before we leave, Mr. H ushers my father into the kitchen and hands him a check. My father, always so tall and straight, is slumped. I watch him shake Mr. H's hand. For a second, I feel like I don't know my own dad.

As we're waiting out in the hall for the elevator, Nicolas comes over to us, looking serious.

"Hey, Destiny. Can I talk to you?"

"Uh, sure." I glance at my parents. "I'll take the bus home, okay?"

"Make sure she gets on the bus," my dad tells Nicolas. Nicolas nods.

My parents kiss me, and America watches closely as Nicolas and I go out the door to the stairwell. We sit on the concrete steps under the EXIT sign. He's quiet, staring down at his sneakers. I'm so happy he wants to talk to me alone that I put my hand on his knee without even thinking.

"What's up?" I say.

He looks at me like he's about to say something, then stops and just grins.

"Did you ever finish that paper on the Harlem Renaissance?" I ask, breaking the silence.

"I haven't written a single sentence yet," he answers. "Can I borrow your brain?"

"Only if you promise to wash it before you return it."

"Hand wash?" he asks.

"Dry clean only," I say.

We laugh and I push into him, and we just start talking. Not about anything in particular, just random stuff, and it feels really good to be with him, laughing. No pressure.

But then he stops and stares into my eyes. He's just staring at me, and I think maybe he wants to kiss me. So I lean toward him, but instead of leaning toward me, he bends over and tightens his shoelaces.

It is possibly the most embarrassing moment of my ENTIRE FREAKING LIFE!

My face falls on the floor and rolls down the stairs and

right into traffic where it gets run over for not seeing the obvious. Man! I feel like Omar that day by the C train, slapping himself on the forehead and whispering, "¡Estúpido!"

Nicolas straightens up after tightening his laces. I look up and down the stairwell, hoping no one catches me sitting there in my pool of rejection.

"I—"

"Look—"

"I'm—"

"I thought—"

"We're friends, right Destiny?" he asks.

OMG! Did he just "friend" me?

I want to ask him if he gives all of his "friends" intense massages and long funny looks, but I don't.

"Yeah," I say as reality slams down on me. "Of course. Of course we're friends. I mean, we've only really seen each other about three times. I mean, that's hardly a friendship . . . I mean . . . it's a start but . . . of course we're friends."

"I've been thinking about the whole *quince* thing," says Nicolas.

I hold my breath.

Maybe he's not friending me?

Then he adds, "If you still want me to go to your *quince*, that's cool. It's good to have your friends around for stuff like that."

My breath whooshes out, like a balloon that's deflated. "Sure, that would be great."

I almost add "dude" at the end. Erin would be proud. But I feel like I'm going to faint right there on the stairs.

"Hey, are you okay?" Nicolas asks, and he sounds like he's actually concerned. "You look kinda sick."

"I'm fine. At school my nickname is *corazón de piedra*."

"You have a heart of stone?"

"Not really. But I'm working on it."

Nicolas and I laugh again. But there isn't really anything funny about it. It's probably the worst thing that could ever happen, getting friended by a boy you like under an EXIT sign. (Okay, getting shot is probably worse, but still.)

We talk a bit more about nothing and finally say goodnight, and I rush out of Yasmin's building just in time to catch the bus on the corner. I think of Nicolas's promise to my dad and wonder if he's the kind of guy who doesn't keep his word.

When I get home, my family's in the kitchen. My dad's breaking out the Twinkies, my mom's making tea, and America's moping at the kitchen table.

I don't know how much the check was for, but nobody seems happy now that we have it.

My father pulls my mother close and they kiss. Sweetly. And she places her head on his shoulder. Even America doesn't make fun and we're all quiet. . . .

saturday

DEPRESSION

Fog.
Days pass.
Thursday.
Friday.
Breakfast.
School.
Dinner.
Homework.
Night.
Sleep.
Morning.
Repeat.
Fog and more fog.

If I were a baseball player, my batting average would totally suck! I wake up Saturday, really mad at Omar and still completely devastated about Nicolas.

I also feel really, really stupid. All those ideas I had that Nicolas was into me, felt the same way about me as I felt about him. And he's just thinking of me as a friend. Or worse, he's just a huge flirt! And the truth is, I don't know him at all. None of it was real!

I'm lying in bed, staring up at the ceiling, not knowing what to do. I thought I'd feel better by the weekend, but it's the opposite. *Quinceañera.* High school. Who cares?

I drag myself into the kitchen, and my mother immediately hands me a pen and my *quince* invitations. I scowl a scowl that America would envy.

"I want you to start working on your *quince* speech this weekend," she tells me. "I'm going to buy gifts for your court and meet with a salsa band and a choreographer for your waltz tomorrow, so you *must* pick your *chambelanes* and *damas* by Monday. And, never mind what your sister says, in the first week of October, I made our appointment to alter your dress."

My dad's drinking coffee at the table.

"Leave her alone, *querida*. She just woke up," he says, and my mom declares, "Never."

I slump into a chair. My dad starts telling stories about me as a little kid to cheer me up. Back when all the boys used to love me and all my luck was good. Yeah, right.

My sister comes in, yawning loudly.

"You remember our Christmas party when you were five, Destiny?" my father asks.

"I remember," I say. My parents actually throw great parties in our apartment—lots of good food, music, and dancing—and I remember all of them. My *quince* would be so much simpler if they did it that way. No worries about rent or loans or layoffs. But then it wouldn't be a super-impressive event like Yasmin's.

"The party where Mr. Rojas sat you on his lap—" my dad continues.

"That sounds perverted," America interrupts.

"America!" my mother protests. "Mr. Rojas played the organ at Our Lady of Perpetual Sorrow for years."

"Ay." My father smiles. "He was a terrible organ player. But he had a gift for seeing the future. He said you would break a lot of hearts when you grew up."

Ha. Some gift, Mr. Rojas.

"He loved to joke," my dad says. "He asked you to marry him. Everyone looked at you and you said, so serious, 'But when I'm old enough to marry you, you'll be dead, Mr. Rojas.' You couldn't understand why everyone was laughing. The point is, Mr. Rojas saw something special in you. And he's never wrong about those things."

America says to my mother, "Papi's so good to us. Where did you find him?"

"On my doorstep one morning, rolled up in *La Prensa*."

La Prensa is like the Latino *Daily News*. My mother and father make their love eyes at each other. After almost twenty years of marriage? Horndogs!

I can't cheer up.

After breakfast, my father offers to take us all to the movies. That's what he does when he knows that one of us is bummed out, and it usually makes us feel better. America's been down since the whole Tomas/Bala thing, but she perks up as she grabs my father's newspaper from the kitchen table to see what's playing. I try and get into the spirit because I know everyone wants me to feel better (even though they don't know about Nicolas), but it's no use.

"I just need to take my board out for a spin and I'll be fine," I say. Anyway, the last thing I need is to worry about how much it'd cost to take us all out to the movies.

My dad eyes me skeptically. "Are you sure, *nena*?"

I nod.

"You can get a large popcorn all for yourself," my mom offers.

"Hey!" America looks up from the newspaper. "If she gets one, I get one!"

"You don't need the extra calories," my mom assures her, clearing the table.

America gasps. "You didn't just say that!"

My mother smiles sweetly and pinches her cheek. "Oh yes, I did."

But not even the lure of buttery, popped goodness is enough to tempt me. How depressing is that?

Outside, I roll fast on my board to Columbus Avenue, thinking about Erin and Stephanie. I love them, but Stephanie's never been dumped in her life, and Erin's never had anyone who could dump her—as if anyone would dare to try. I just want to avoid everybody.

Then I see Omar across the street.

"Hey, Destiny!"

He rushes across the road. I try to roll around him, but he blocks me.

"C'mon, just let me explain—"

I let loose, "There's nothing to explain! You did an incredibly sneaky—"

"But I didn't do it to be sneaky, I swear!"

"Then why did you do it?"

He just stares at me with this dumb expression on his face.

"I'm out of here." I jump off my board and stomp away so hard I almost break my ankle.

He doesn't even try to stop me.

I ride to the band shell in the middle of Central Park. It's an outdoor concert stage in the shape of a seashell where they play music in the summer. The shell is empty. I take a board and some bricks and set up a small ramp and practice doing tiny jumps. I only fall two hundred times, almost sprain my ankle three hundred times, almost break four hundred bones, and the echoes of my falls in the shell only reach as far as the West Side Highway. Not bad.

I'm starving, so I go to Chipotle on Broadway and spend some of my Peter babysitting money on a burrito and then I go to Pinkberry on Amsterdam and get a large cup of whatever that yogurty stuff is (I like to call it sweet creamy heaven, but that's me).

Alone.

I've always thought that people who eat alone are lonely, but it actually cheers me up a bit. I don't have to talk to anyone. I can just sit and eat and walk and eat and think and eat, which is all I feel like doing anyway.

But during my little pity party, I realize I need to come

up with a way to make some more money. Not just a little money—enough to pay for the whole Sweet 15. Then my dad wouldn't have to use that check from Mr. Hernandez, and my parents wouldn't be so stressed out. We could go back to our usual level of Mami and America bickering, which is looking pretty good right about now.

How could I ever earn that much money by next month?

I finish my sweet creamy heaven and head home. All I want to do is hide in my room and watch TV.

When I get in the apartment, I can hear Barry White playing from my parents' bedroom and we all know what that means, so I go to my room and search the Internet and then look through every book on my shelf, trying to find the answer for how to solve all of my problems.

Nothing.

I look at the TV.

No answers there.

I grab *When I Was Puerto Rican* by Esmerelda Santiago off my shelf. America comes in, throws herself down on the bed beside me, and begins playing with my hair.

"Destiny Lozada is depressed today," she sings.

"Destiny Lozada isn't anything today. Destiny Lozada just is," I tell her.

"How very existential. Are you still mad about Omar and the Skate15 thing?"

"He finally does something unpredictable and that's what I get."

"It was mom who put Omar up to it, you know."

"Huh?"

"Mom didn't actually tell him to become Skate Fifteen. But she's the one who got it into his head that you would maybe consider him as your *caballero* and that he should get it together and do something exciting and romantic. So he probably went home and watched some *telenovela* and then a bit of *Titanic* and came up with his Skate Fifteen alter ego."

"I can't believe it." Except I can.

"Well," says America, "forget that. There's a bigger picture. You did a great job stalling on the dress alteration. The Jezebels and I are meeting to put together a stronger case against the dress and the heels thing this time, so don't you worry. Help is on the way. The fight is still on!"

"I don't care anymore," I grumble.

"Hey, Dusty, do me a favor?" she asks.

"What?"

"Cheer up, for God's sake!"

"Jeez." I knock myself softly on the forehead. "You're absolutely right. What was I thinking?"

My sister kisses my forehead and leaves me to have some more "alone time."

I think again about ways to make money. All I can come up with is babysitting and maybe giving skateboarding lessons to little kids in my building, but how much could I earn? I lie back on my bed and sing along to the saddest Selena song I can find on an old CD that Maritza gave me. When that gets boring, I go back to my computer and write some poetry, the "Love Sucks" kind.

Let the rain fall down on me
Like tears I want to cry

Washing all the sad off me
The sad that fills my eyes
Love. What is it good for?
Absolutely nothing

Okay. So I'm no Sylvia Plath.

I'm even depressing Natasha and Fuzzy. They're both watching me from the corner of my bed with "sad-filled" eyes. Natasha, I understand. She's always been sensitive to my moods. But Fuzzy? That's serious. It isn't easy to depress a stuffed orange bear.

I'm going for the remote when my cell rings. My stomach drops to my knees. Maybe it's Nicolas!

I check to see who's calling, but I don't recognize the number.

"Hello?"

"Hi, it's Yasmin."

Yasmin? I sit up on my bed.

"Hi."

I pull Natasha and Fuzzy close.

"I just wanted to say," she tells me, "that I think my cousin Nicolas is a total dog."

"What do you mean?" I play with Natasha's whiskers.

"Nicolas is going out with Amanda, but he told me that he's been hanging out with you, too. And that he likes you," Yasmin adds.

He likes me? I knew it! I'm not nuts.

Not totally, anyway. He's going out with Amanda??

"So," I ask, all casual, "Nicolas said he was crazy about me?"

"I don't know about 'crazy,' but he told me that he likes you and he was planning on making some kind of move."

"What kind of move?" I ask, even more casually. "When did he tell you this?"

"It doesn't matter, right?"

"No," I agree. "Of course it doesn't matter."

But it kind of does.

"I told him to cut it out and leave you alone, or I would tell Amanda what he was up to. He told me to mind my own business. So I told Amanda. She thought I was just nuts or something, or that I thought my family was better than hers and didn't want her seeing my cousin. And suddenly, I was the school slut. Just like that."

Natasha stretches out on the pillow beside me. I want to ask Yasmin if any of the rumors are true, but it doesn't exactly feel like the right time.

"Amanda told Nicolas what I said about him," Yasmin goes on. "Now everybody's mad at me. That's why I was pissed at dinner. That's why Nicolas wasn't talking to me. I don't care. I didn't do anything wrong."

"Wow."

"Yeah," says Yasmin. "I'm not trying to butt in. It's just not right. Nicolas did the same kind of stuff in Philadelphia. He bragged about it to me."

I want to feel great about Nicolas liking me but how can I, knowing that he's going out with someone else and totally lying to her?

"Not cool," I say.

"I wanted to tell you before but . . ."

"Thanks. I'm glad you told me now."

"I just thought you should know. . . ."

Silence.

Then: "Your *quince* is coming up soon, huh?" she asks.

"Next month."

More silence.

"Well, good luck. See you in drama," she says.

"Yeah. See you."

I hang up the phone. What did she mean by wishing me good luck? Is she making fun of the fact that my parents borrowed money from her parents? Or am I being crazy? It was nice of her to call. Even if it hurts. I'm so tired of being silent and passive about my *quince*. It's getting me—and my whole family—absolutely nowhere. And I feel all alone in this mess. (Sorry, Natasha. Sorry, Fuzz. It's not your fault.) It's like I'm caught in between, like I'm in limbo somewhere between junior high and high school, between the US and Puerto Rico, between my sister and my mother, between being a snotty little kid and a smart young woman.

But I could never cancel the *quince*. I just couldn't do that to my mother.

Could I?

monday

THE SLAP

As I walk into drama class, there's Mr. Porton talking to Yasmin. He's probably telling her how great she's been doing. But I can't help thinking of the rumors.

I sit down, and Mr. Porton announces, "We're going to do improvs based on scenes from famous movies. Two characters. Extreme weather conditions as one of your obstacles. Who's up first?"

"I'll go!" Yasmin volunteers.

"Anybody else?" asks Mr. Porton. "Anybody? C'mon."

He scans the room. Nobody raises their hand, probably because of Yasmin's slut status.

I feel weird after that call from Yasmin. There she is with her freckles and reddish hair and low-cut blouse and jeans so far down her hips that her bellybutton shows, and I feel as half-naked as she looks because of how much she knows about me, my family, my *quince*, and the borrowed money. But it was really nice of her to tell me about Nicolas . . . so I raise my hand.

"Come on up, Destiny." Mr. Porton waves me over. "You guys can pick the scene."

I jump up on the stage.

"What do you want to do?" I ask Yasmin as we huddle in a corner.

Yasmin glances over my shoulder, and her eyes light up. I look back and see the giant standing fan near the door of the theater.

"Do you know *Fatal Attraction*?" Yasmin asks. "We could do an improv about the wife and the obsessed woman that the stupid husband has an affair with . . . stuck in a hurricane."

"That's good!"

Yasmin and I drag the fan to one end of the stage, and we walk to the opposite end. Yasmin asks Mr. Porton to switch on the fan when we signal him.

"Now!"

Mr. Porton switches the fan on full blast, and it starts blowing my hair all over the place. The fan keeps blowing and my hair keeps flying and pretty soon, I just don't care anymore and I totally give in to it. Yasmin does, too, and we're completely playing off of each other, walking in the direction of the blowing fan.

"Stay away from my husband!" I yell.

"It's not your husband I'm after!" Yasmin yells back. "It's your rabbit!"

"Don't you dare touch my rabbit!"

"I'm going to your house right now to boil your rabbit!"

Yasmin moves in slow motion ahead of me. I move in slow motion, too, as if I'm trying to catch her but can't.

"Take my husband!" I yell. "Take my husband! But don't touch my rabbit!"

Everyone's laughing hysterically and when we're finished,

Mr. Porton says, "That was inspired. Great job!"

Man, that feels good!

We sit down, and Yasmin tells me, "You were awesome."

"No!" I correct her. "*You* were awesome!"

I'm embarrassed that I've been thinking trash about Yasmin and here she is, being so nice to me again. It goes to show, you never know a person until you get to know them, even if you thought you knew them. (You can quote me on that.) A.K.A., don't judge a girl by her reputation.

When the bell rings, Amanda walks by me and says, "That was pretty cool." I'm so shocked, I don't know how to respond. I nod and walk out with Yasmin. We go downstairs to our lockers and as I'm opening mine, I hear, "Hey, Destiny!"

I turn around. Great. It's Amanda again. She's with Melanie, and they're both looking unhappy.

"Yes?"

"Are you too good for me?" hisses Amanda, putting her hands on her skinny hips and flipping her blonde hair back. "I said that what you did was cool. You can't say thank you?"

"Thank you," I say tightly.

Amanda sucks her teeth. "Is every girl in this school either a slut or a retard?" she asks Melanie.

"Leave her alone," says Yasmin.

Amanda looks Yasmin up and down. "Stay out of this, traitor."

"Real mature, Amanda," says Yasmin.

"Oh, what're you, like, her best friend now?" Amanda sounds kind of hurt.

"What would you know about best friends?" Yasmin asks.

"You're the one who was supposed to be my friend," Amanda says. "Not talk crap about my boyfriend, just because you don't have one of your own."

"I told you the truth," snaps Yasmin. "Nicolas is my cousin, and I'm telling you he's playing with you."

Amanda gazes down at the floor as if she's considering the truth of Yasmin's words.

Yasmin asks softly, "Aren't you tired of being treated like crap by him?"

Amanda looks up at Yasmin and then at me and back at Yasmin, and her bottom lip trembles. She gets this awful wounded look on her face for a second, like she's actually going to cry.

Then Amanda pulls herself together and sneers at Yasmin. "Slut!"

Yasmin flinches like she's been hit. I notice Melanie is running up the stairs.

"Nicolas is the slut!" Yasmin screams in Amanda's face.

Amanda pushes Yasmin against a locker, and Yasmin pushes her, too. The noise of their backs slamming against the lockers is so loud you'd swear somebody is getting killed.

Amanda raises her fist as if to hit Yasmin for real.

"Don't!" I grab Amanda's wrist, and she glares at me like I'm next, and that's when Mr. Porton comes running down into the basement, with Melanie right behind him, yelling, "Girls! Girls!"

Too late! Amanda raises her other fist at me, and suddenly my hand comes out of nowhere and slaps Amanda across the mouth.

She gasps. Blood trickles from her lip.

"You hit me!" she cries, like she can't believe it.

I can't believe it, either. I have never slapped anybody in my entire life. I'm just not a violent person. And hitting somebody is not like in the movies where you just hear a crack or the comic books where you see BAM! or WAP! in giant red letters. In real life, it's much more intense. I can feel the sting of her face on my hand. And hear the echo of the slap, like raw chicken being slammed down on a kitchen counter. Amanda just stands there, touching her bloody lip. Yasmin looks a little shocked herself.

There's total silence in the basement until Mr. Porton yells, "DESTINY!"

10 minutes later

DEAN MARKOFF AND THE APOLOGY

There's a strict NO FIGHTING policy at Columbus Prep, so Yasmin, Amanda, and I are all taken to the dean's office like a line of prisoners. We sit outside on wooden chairs with Mr. Porton as our security guard. Erin and Stephanie pop their heads in, their eyes all bugged out.

"What the heck happened?" says Erin.

"Are you okay?" asks Stephanie.

"Girls, go to your class!" orders Mr. Porton. He seems totally different in this situation. Even his man-purse looks angry.

"The whole school is talking," says Stephanie.

Erin nods. "Even the seniors."

I wonder how long it'll take to reach my sister.

"I'll talk to you guys later," I tell my friends.

Stephanie puts her hand on my shoulder. "Do you want us to—"

"Class!" Mr. Porton barks. "Now!"

Erin takes off. Stephanie sashays out.

I'm sent into the dean's office first.

I sit there with my head bowed. Dean Markoff says, "This is so out of character for you, Destiny. I am really disappointed."

I'm trying to act all cool, but honestly, I'm ashamed. More than I thought I would be. Dean Markoff is peering straight at me—through me, in fact—with these big blue cat eyes that remind me of Natasha's. I can't escape, no matter where I look.

"Are you under stress at home?" she asks.

"No," I lie.

"You're a smart girl who knows better than to use violence to solve a problem."

"Amanda was going to hit me first. She started it by calling Yasmin a slut."

"Do you know what that word means?"

I nod my head. Who doesn't?

"Well, I don't think everyone fully realizes its implications, why it's wrong to use that kind of word against another girl."

"I think I do."

"That's good, Destiny. This word is so damaging to a young woman's self-esteem. I wish you wouldn't use it against each other."

There's a knock on the door, and in walk my parents. I have to sit through another fifteen minutes of shame as Dean Markoff tells them what happened.

And it doesn't end there. I have to join Issues Group, which is a counseling thing run by a social worker that meets once a week after school. The usual reasons kids get sent to Issues Group are: cutting class, vandalism, fighting, doing drugs or drinking, and suicide attempts. (And if you attempt suicide after fighting and drinking and drugging while cutting class and committing vandalism, you'll probably have to go to Issues Group for the rest of your life.)

My mother shudders and shakes her head at the word "counseling," and between her clicking tongue and my father staring silently and rubbing on his goatee, I feel like crawling under the desk. The dean's disappointment is nothing compared to the way they're looking at me.

As we drive home, my mom says to my father, "If it wasn't for that loan from Julia and all of the deposits, I swear, I'd cancel her *quince*."

Cancel my *quince*? I didn't think I'd ever hear her say those words. She really is upset.

"I don't think that's necessary," my father says. "But no TV, Destiny. No skateboarding. No Internet except for homework. For one month. You can have a little break on the weekends, but you come straight home after school."

He is so calm but so serious. I think of the summer when I was eight, and the Hernandezes rented a house with a pool in the Berkshires, and we stayed for a week. I was learning to swim with a Winnie-the-Pooh plastic-bubble-thing around my waist. I'd jump off the side of the pool and into my father's arms. And he'd catch me. Over and over. I jumped too far one time and kicked him in the face, and you know what my father did? *Nada.* It was an accident but still, if it had been my mother, I think she would've had me arrested for assault. That's my dad. Always calm.

Mami's normal voice is so loud that when she gets angry it's not very different, but when my father gets angry, it's real quiet and serious. And then the anger's gone, just as quickly as it came. Somehow, though, it hurts more.

My mother tries to calm down, but she can't hold herself back anymore. "Your father and I had to leave work, Destiny! And we had to sit in that woman's office, listening to her talk about our daughter like you're some kind of juvenile delinquent! How do you think this makes Latinos look?"

Am I supposed to be responsible for every Latino now? I stare out the car window. I see the green trees and gray boulders of Central Park West, and I can hear the band shell calling me.

"They think we raised a girl who doesn't know how to act. You're on scholarship there, don't you forget that. You want to get kicked out, is that it, Destiny?"

"Mami," I say, "I'm not proud of what happened, but it was Amanda who started it. She's such a spoiled little jerk. Maybe she deserves—"

"Destiny." My father looks at me in the rearview mirror.

My mother whirls around. "You're not in a gang, are you?"

"No, Mami. There are no gangs at Columbus Prep. Unless you count the chess club."

"Thank God!"

"You must apologize to her, Destiny," my father states.

I hold my breath. My dad doesn't lay down the law often but when he does, it's unheard of to go against him. Even America doesn't dare.

"I can't," I say weakly.

My father pulls over and stops the car. My mother is silent for once.

"What do you mean?" he asks quietly. Too quietly.

"Well . . . Amanda should really be apologizing to Yasmin."

My dad doesn't say anything, so I continue, "She called Yasmin names, and she was going to hit me first, I just beat her to it."

My father nods to let me know he's listening. I get a little bolder.

"So really, I just defended myself *and* Yasmin. Amanda deserved it."

When I see my father's expression, my face falls. He's not angry, just sad.

He puts up his hand. "If you apologize to Amanda, it must be because you know that doing so would make you a better person. And not better than Amanda, better than what you thought you could be. But I don't want to force you, Destiny. If you want, we can go home and you don't have to apologize and I will never mention it again. Or we can go visit Amanda later, and you can apologize for your part in this mess. You choose."

We sit there in the car. Waiting for me to decide.

We don't have to wait long.

"I want to be a better person," I say.

That night, at Amanda's building on 90th Street and Riverside Drive, we can't find parking so my father stays in the car with the motor running like a bank robber. The lobby is like a

French palace, with white marble floors, chandeliers, golden elevators, glass walls, a fountain, and a waiting area with white leather couches and a white marble coffee table. Mrs. H would like it. Amanda and her mother are called downstairs by the doorman. They get off the elevator and walk into the lobby. Amanda's mom is really thin, and she's wearing a white silk blouse with this jeweled pin that looks like a giant bug. When she sees me and my mom, she gives us a bright painted-on smile.

Amanda doesn't. She stares at me like I'm crazy. "What're you doing here?"

I almost can't do it, but then I see my dad waiting outside, and I know I have to.

"I came over to apologize," I tell her.

"Oh?" Amanda folds her arms.

"I'm sorry," I say as quickly as possible.

"Shake her hand," my mother suggests to me.

I go to shake Amanda's hand, but she folds her arms tighter.

"Girls shouldn't fight," Amanda's mother scolds both of us.

"Talk next time," adds my mother.

"Shake her hand," hisses Amanda's mom. Now that she's closer, I realize she smells like alcohol.

Amanda reluctantly shakes my hand.

"Thank you so much for coming," her mother says. "Frankly, I'm surprised she didn't get more than a slap. My daughter's a bit of a bully. She gets it from her father."

"Mom!" Amanda looks mortified.

"Shut up!" Her mother flicks Amanda's cheek with one long, polished nail. Amanda's cheeks go red, and not just from her mother's nail. I always thought Amanda had it made, but now she seems so miserable. I almost feel bad we came.

"You don't know what this girl has put me through since my divorce," her mother tells us.

"They're still children. . . ." says my mother. "She's having a hard time?"

"Amanda's been having a hard time for too many years," her mother snorts. I notice her hands are trembling. "Her father's fighting me for every cent, and he never seems to find the time to see his precious daughter. I keep getting complaints from a school that I'm paying a fortune to—"

"You're embarrassing me," Amanda whimpers.

"You're embarrassing yourself!"

They glare at each other.

"Well," says my mom after about a year of uncomfortable silence. "Maybe it's good that they're all going to counseling."

"I wouldn't hold my breath." Amanda's mom snorts again.

My mother looks at me sympathetically, like she might just have an idea where this fight came from. "It's getting late. We better go."

I'm feeling pretty lucky about having the parents I do.

"Thank you for coming!" Amanda's mother is all smiles again and shakes our hands. "It was a pleasure meeting you both."

"Ah, yes, you too," my mother agrees. "Good-bye, Amanda."

"The lady is talking to you, Amanda!"

"Good-bye," says Amanda in a hollow voice.

She stands there with her eyes closed as we leave. It's like she's not really Amanda anymore. She's like a ghost.

As we get back into the car, my father nods at me. I'm not sure if I feel like a better person, but I know that I'm glad I apologized.

I feel free, like I'm sure about what's important and what's not and what love is and what it's not and what I want to do.

And I say it out loud. Finally. "I'm canceling my *quinceañera*."

ACT FOUR

friday

ISSUES

So.

Yasmin, Amanda, and I have Issues Group with Mrs. Diamant (who happens to be married to my history teacher, Mr. Diamant). She's a social worker with the energy of a gym teacher, in jeans and a turquoise blouse, with porcelain skin, intense eyes, and wild black hair that could almost compete with America's.

Issues Group meets every Friday until the end of this semester. There are ten other students in the group, mostly older guys. We're sitting in the chemistry lab on uncomfortable plastic chairs arranged in a circle. Yasmin is on my right (wearing old jeans and a simple striped T-shirt with nothing extra hanging out today). Amanda is two seats over on my left, all in black as if she's at her own funeral. The room smells like sulfur. We each say our name in a monotone. No one looks anyone else in the eye.

"Okay!" Mrs. Diamant slaps her knees. "Now that we've introduced ourselves, I want you all to understand that I am here to listen and stay open to your problems, thoughts, opinions, and goals. That's why Issues Group was created. So for now, let's go around the room, and I want everyone to share a thought or a feeling or something they want to change about themselves. And don't say underwear!"

We all stare blankly at her.

"I'll go first," she continues, still very chipper. "Let's see . . . I'm thinking that you are all very brave for coming here." (Did we have a choice?) "I'm feeling hopeful and I want us all to do good work together." Mrs. Diamant scans the room. "But we have to get to know each other, so . . ."

She gestures at Yasmin.

"Yasmin! Why don't you go first? What's going on with you? What do you want from the group?"

Yasmin pulls on her hair and glances at Amanda and then at me.

"Well . . . I think I'm feeling . . . misunderstood this year, and I feel . . ." Her voice drops. "I want people to really see who I am and not who they want me to be. I want to stop trying to be who I'm not so that people will like me."

I'm impressed by her honesty. It's like whatever Yasmin does, her insides don't match her outsides and people just don't get her.

"Thank you, Yasmin," says Mrs. Diamant. "Being ourselves and being seen for who we really are isn't easy."

Mrs. Diamant's intense eyes land on me. "Destiny?"

I'm not ready! Why didn't I plan an answer?

"Um . . ." Before I can think, I hear my voice forging on. "I never really thought of myself as a judgmental person, but I am. I'm feeling pretty crappy about that, and I want to . . . to start thinking for myself more, I guess. I want to stop being so quiet about what I want and what I need."

Mrs. Diamant nods enthusiastically. "That's great, Destiny. Can you tell us how that's manifesting in your life, not thinking for yourself and not saying what you need?"

She didn't ask Yasmin any extra questions, why is she asking me?

"Uh, I'm not sure. With family and friends, I guess."

"You know, Destiny, the farther we push things down, the more they surface."

Mrs. Diamant is staring at me, sort of kindly and gently, with those all-knowing eyes and, I don't know, I'm just so tired of keeping in all these thoughts that have been racing around in my brain and I start talking.

"I used to think that if you had a lot of money, or more than most, that you were automatically happy."

I look at Yasmin and Amanda.

"Now I know that's not true. Everybody has their problems. In my family, everyone has an opinion of what they think I should do, and I never question it. I try not to make trouble. I watch TV. I talk to my pets." (I don't mention one is a stuffed bear.) "Like this *quinceañera* I wouldn't mind having so much, except that I was being torn in half by my mother and my sister, and my parents weren't telling me the truth about the costs. The *quinceañera* was taking over every part of my life, like some kind of disease. So I canceled it. I did that. Me."

I take a breath. "I'm tired of feeling helpless and acting helpless and saying nothing when I want to say so much."

Mrs. Diamant is nodding like crazy. Everyone in the room is staring at me. Then, slowly, they all nod their heads, too.

Including Amanda. It's wild! They're actually getting what I'm saying. Yasmin reaches over and touches my arm for a moment.

Geez, who needs Nicolas Hernandez's incredible massages when I have Issues Group?

Ha!

After Issues Group, I go straight home as instructed and start on my homework. My mom calls me out of my room for dinner. The doorbell rings. She smiles suspiciously and tells me to answer it. I open the front door, and there he is again.

"What're you doing here?" I ask.

Nicolas shrugs. "Your mom invited me."

"What?"

"She called my aunt and said that maybe you'd change your mind about canceling your *quince* if I'd be your *caballero* and invited me to dinner."

"And you came because you want to be my *caballero* so badly?" I ask.

"Well," says Nicolas, "she asked if I needed any help with homework or anything, and I said I had that Harlem Renaissance paper due next week that I haven't even started yet. She can be pretty persuasive."

He doesn't know the half of it. After I canceled my *quince*, she threatened to put me up for adoption . . . in Romania!

"So, you want me to help you write your paper, is that it?" I can hardly believe the words coming out of my mouth. It's like Issues Group has unleashed my inner America.

Nicolas shrugs again. "That, and a free dinner." He grins at me, but I fight the urge to grin back.

"Destiny!" my mother shrieks from the kitchen. "Why are you and Nicolas out in the hallway? Invite him in—he's our guest."

I let Nicolas in. He's carrying a book bag and wearing a red T-shirt and blue jeans and looks as good as ever, unfortunately.

"I'm going to study with Hailey and Maritza." America rushes toward the front door with her bag and a stack of books. She wants no part of whatever it is that's about to go down.

"Not before you eat your dinner," scolds my mother.

"I'm not hungry."

"I made my spaghetti."

America blinks. "I guess I can stay."

My mother's spaghetti *is* amazing. She makes the sauce with three different kinds of cheese and a secret spice, and if Nicolas weren't here, I'd be really excited myself.

My dad quietly sizes up Nicolas.

"How strong are you, Nicolas?" Mami asks.

Huh? Where's this going?

"Uh . . . I'm pretty strong, I guess."

It turns out Nicolas is very strong. He helps my father open a window in the kitchen that's been stuck for like three hundred years, but before he can get to the second window, my mother grabs Nicolas, pulls back a chair, and pushes him into it.

It's time for spaghetti. America glares at Nicolas between

bites. I didn't tell any of them about Nicolas having a girlfriend, but I know America has a bad feeling about him. My father just sips his red wine.

"Destiny has canceled her *quince*," my mother announces, as if we don't know already. "What a handsome *caballero* Nicolas would have made!"

Nicolas is looking right at me with those amazing brown eyes and his mysterious little smile. I feel like I'm still trying to figure him out, even now. I just never know what to expect from him, and there's something exciting about that. He starts talking about how he misses his family and how his sister had a *quinceañera* in Philadelphia and it was a blast and that if I decide to have one again, he can do the *caballero* thing, *no problema*. Of course, he mentions nothing about his girlfriend, Amanda, and how we would go only as "friends."

"How sweet of you, Nicolas." My mom beams her eyes at me like lasers. "We'll certainly keep that in mind."

Then she's off on her "we shouldn't forget our roots" thing. Nicolas keeps nodding sweetly until I say, "Careful, Nicolas, or your head's going to fall off."

Everybody stares at me. I don't know who's more surprised, them or me.

Nicolas looks a little freaked out and stuffs his face with spaghetti.

My mother pauses and changes tactics. "So, Nicolas, what are your goals?"

"I dunno," Nicolas mumbles, his mouth full of sauce. "I like to skate. I'm learning stuff on computers. That's alright."

"Ah!" Mami says. "Computers? You can make a good career in computers."

So that's it! My mother is pushing for Nicolas to be my *caballero* because she sees him as another potential computer genius, since he's a Hernandez and they're rich from computers, and maybe it runs in his blood or something.

America opens her mouth as if she's about to protest but I take charge.

"He didn't say he wants a career in computers," I tell my mom.

"He didn't say he *doesn't* want a career in computers. Have you ever been to Puerto Rico, Nicolas?"

"No, ma'am."

"Ma'am," my mother repeats and turns to me. "See how polite?"

"All my friends are polite," I say. "This must be so much fun for you, Nicolas."

Nicolas looks at my father for help, but my dad sips his red wine.

"Nicolas is having a wonderful time." My mother shreds a little more parmesan on his spaghetti. "Besides, I thought we could all help each other."

"We?" I say.

"You get straight A's in English, and he needs help on his paper. One hand washes *la otra.*"

"And how is Nicolas going to wash your hand?" I ask.

My mother turns back to Nicolas. "Did you wear a tuxedo to your sister's *quinceañera*?"

"Yeah. Yes."

"You have a girlfriend, don't you?" I ask him.

America's eyes widen and she opens her mouth again to say something, but I put up my hand and she just glares at Nicolas.

Let's see him get out of this one.

But he must have figured Yasmin told me by now. He just nods his head all cool and slurps his spaghetti.

"Her name is Amanda," I tell my mother. "You met her."

"Amanda?" my mother repeats, confused.

America shakes her head like she knew it all along.

"But Amanda'll understand it's just a friend thing if Destiny wants to do it," Nicolas adds, his mouth smeared with sauce.

"Will she really?" I say.

Mami looks like she wants to strangle herself with a strand of spaghetti. "Oh," she says. "Well, a *caballero* can be just a friend."

Silence. We all eat.

I feel bad for my mom. She still wants me to have this perfect *quinceañera*, but it isn't going to happen. And I need to figure out how to make her understand so she'll start canceling stuff, including Mrs. H's loan. The dress hasn't been altered so returning it shouldn't be a problem. But there are all the other deposits that we need to try and get back as soon as possible.

At the end of the meal, when my mom goes to make some coffee, I say quickly, "Nicolas and I should go talk about his paper." I don't know why, but I feel like I should still help him, like it's the right thing to do.

In my room, Nicolas and I sit on the floor, with the door open, and Mami keeps popping in to make sure we have everything we need. We're reading over the assignment sheet from his English class, and he's sort of leaning in toward me. He smells like bubble gum, and his bare arm is touching mine.

"Why don't you try writing a paper on this question?" I ask, pointing to #3 on the sheet.

"I'm more interested in that one." His finger is pointing to #4, but he's staring at me.

"What were three major events that gave rise to the Harlem Renaissance?" I read aloud, then I glance at him. He's still staring at me.

"You shouldn't pull your hair back all the time," he says. "Didn't we talk about that?"

"I like it this way."

He puts his hand on my knee. "Massage?"

I remove his hand from my knee.

"Why you so tense?" he asks.

"We're in my bedroom, on the floor, and my mom is popping in and out like it's Groundhog Day, and you have a girlfriend so I'm not sure why you're touching me."

He frowns. "We're friends, right?"

"I thought we were. That's what you said you wanted."

"It *is* what I want."

"So why are you touching me like that if we're just friends?"

"Relax," he whispers in my ear, and as soon as he says it, I push him away.

"Go!" I tell him, jumping up. "Just go."
He shrugs and grabs his school stuff.
"Sorry," he says.
And Nicolas goes.
Just like that.

1 week later

MY FRIEND YASMIN

In our next Issues Group, Mrs. Diamant, wearing a funky gray suit jacket, begins by saying, "Let me ask you all a question. What is conflict?"

We wait to see who will volunteer the answer. Amanda raises her hand.

"Yes!" Mrs. Diamant points at her.

"When people disagree?" asks Amanda. She flips back her hair and checks her watch like she's bored already. I think of the scene in her lobby last week and wonder how much of her attitude is an act.

Mrs. Diamant nods. "Exactly! Conflict means I want something; you want something else. Who will get what they want?"

Maybe I could bring America and my mother in for show-and-tell.

"Amanda, do me a favor, step into the middle of the circle and . . ."

Mrs. Diamant scans the room with her piercing eyes, and to my absolute horror, they land on me. "Destiny, will you join her? What I'd like is for each of you to put six chairs in the middle of the circle."

I make my way around the room with Amanda, grabbing chairs and carrying them into the middle of the circle. Everyone's watching like we're performing this amazing feat, but we're just dragging chairs and I feel really awkward, especially because I have no idea what Nicolas has told Amanda about me.

"Thank you," says Mrs. Diamant.

Amanda is shaking her head like that's the dumbest thing she's ever done, but she doesn't ask any questions.

I'm tired of not asking questions. "What are these chairs for?"

"They're an exercise in conflict," Mrs. Diamant answers with a broad smile.

I try to nod patiently.

"Now, Amanda, I want you to start stacking the chairs. Go ahead." Amanda begins to stack the chairs, one on top of the other.

"And Destiny, I want you to keep them unstacked."

Amanda keeps stacking but I'm frozen, unsure what to do. I look at Mrs. Diamant.

"Amanda wants to stack the chairs, and you want to keep them unstacked. Can you stop her?" she asks me.

Amanda reaches for a chair and puts it on top of the other ones. I take it down. She puts it back.

"Okay," says Mrs. Diamant, "the stacking-unstacking thing? Not working so well for you guys, right? Try talking to her, Destiny. Amanda, keep stacking."

"Uh, can you stop doing that, please?"

"Why?" Amanda asks, holding a chair.

"If the chairs are stacked, nobody will be able to sit down, and people need to sit down."

"Well, I don't want anybody to sit down," says Amanda.

"Why not?" I ask.

Amanda shrugs. "If people don't have a place to sit, they won't stay long."

"Why don't you want them to stay?" I ask her.

"Either way they end up leaving."

I know she's talking about her dad. Without us even realizing it, Amanda has stopped stacking.

"Good," says Mrs. Diamant. "The point of this exercise is that communication often removes obstacles. Amanda stopped stacking the chairs after Destiny started questioning her. Communication is the beginning of conflict resolution. And we've begun."

We do a couple more exercises where we get to act out family members (I do a pretty flawless America, if I do say so myself), and then Mrs. Diamant gives us a homework assignment: to work on resolving one major conflict in our life, not by blaming others, but by taking responsibility for our own behavior.

After group, Yasmin is taking her time getting her stuff together, but I wait. "Hey," I say when she looks up, "all that sharing gave me a huge appetite. Do you want to go get a slice?"

"Okay."

"Great."

I call my mother and tell her that I have to talk to Yasmin about something we did in Issues Group (she warns me not to slap anybody, and I promise not to), and Yasmin and I head over toward Broadway.

"How are your classes going?" I ask on the way. I sound like my parents, but I'm nervous.

"Kind of boring. But Art Through Collage with Ms. Eisinger is pretty cool."

"I didn't know you were into art," I say. "What kind of stuff do you do?"

"I'll show you sometime."

Yasmin tucks her hair behind her ears, and I notice that the blue streak is gone.

"Acting and collage are the only places where I can really express myself, you know? I never feel alone when I'm doing that."

"Yeah, I kind of feel like that when I'm skateboarding."

We cross Broadway, past The GAP and swarms of 9-5ers pouring in and out of the subway.

"So what's happening with your *quinceañera*?" Yasmin asks. "I heard about the 'Nicolas to the Rescue' plan. Is it still canceled?"

"Yeah," I say. "My sister's bouncing-off-the-walls happy. My mom, not so much."

We both chuckle. Then Yasmin says, "It's funny, in my family, I don't get much attention. My brothers totally ignored me until my *quince*. Now they're driving the car they gave me, keeping it in Miami until I get my license. Or so they say."

"I know what you mean about being ignored."

"No, your family is different. My party was just about

showing off and being better than anybody. Your family is cool."

"That's one way to put it," I say. "I was thinking of taking playwriting next semester with Mr. Porton and writing a one-act play called *Sweet Fifteen*."

"What'll it be about?" she asks.

"Hmm . . . the story of a Latina named America on the Upper West Side of Manhattan who plots to sabotage every *quinceañera* in the United States and Puerto Rico. It's fictional. Ha!"

"I wish I had a sister," says Yasmin. "Your family always seems so close."

Then it hits me. . . . Yasmin is jealous of my life?

We walk to Famiglia Pizza on 86th Street and order two slices and two Snapples and sit at a table near the back. Yasmin and I devour our slices.

When we're done, she pulls something out of her book bag.

"I made this."

"Wow."

Yasmin has cut out and plastered on a sheet of cardboard different images of females. There are baby girls and young girls and grown women and old women. They are floating in a blue ocean between a map of Puerto Rico and a map of the United States.

"My parents don't exactly get it." She laughs.

"It's about being in the middle," I say.

"What?"

"Your collage." I point. "Do you feel like that? Like you're in America, but you're not. Like you're in Puerto Rico, but you're not? You're somewhere in the middle of the ocean. Lost."

Yasmin sips her Snapple. "Remember the first day of school when I told you that I met this guy in Miami, Julio, and we ended up having sort of a thing? Well, I was pretty depressed after my *quince*, like there was no point to the whole thing, so it was kind of nice to have him to talk to."

"Talk?"

Yasmin makes a face at me. "Yes, Destiny, you can actually have sex with a guy and talk to him, too."

"Sure, yeah, I know. . . . Did you love him?"

"Maybe," she answers. "He was good to me, you know?"

I don't know, but I nod like I do.

I say, "Don't be offended, but can I ask you something?"

"What?"

"Have you slept with a lot of guys at school?" I don't mean for it to come out like that but . . . "If we're going to be friends, I feel like I should know."

"No!" Yasmin shouts. "That was all Amanda, telling everybody lies, so she could get back at me or something. I've only slept with Julio and that was only like two and a half times. And we used protection. I'm not stupid. You don't believe me?"

"No, I do. But . . . I believed the rumors, too. I shouldn't have. I guess I have to take responsibility for that, huh?"

"Issues Group homework!" Yasmin laughs. "Nah, I should have stood up for myself. But who knew it was so easy to go from a nerd to a slut in sixty seconds? All you have to do is make the wrong person mad."

"Yeah." I take a long sip of Snapple. "I like the idea of dating, having fun. But why is everyone in such a rush to have a boyfriend?"

"My mom says when you're a couple it gives you someone else besides your parents to blame for everything."

"What about you?" I say. "Do you want a boyfriend?"

"Me? I guess I'd like to find a guy who treats me with respect and tells me the truth."

"Like Julio?"

"I don't know. I called and e-mailed him a bunch of times. I know he's really busy with school and his mom, but he hasn't texted or e-mailed back, nothing."

"America says you shouldn't waste your time with boys who treat you like crap."

"My mom says the same thing. Then I met Julio and forgot. That's why the Nicolas thing bothered me so much."

Kelly Clarkson's "My Life Would Suck Without You" starts playing over the speakers. Yasmin taps her foot and sways her head to the beat.

"Let's dance!" she says.

"What? In public?"

"There's hardly anybody here."

I look around. Two girls are sitting together, there's a guy on a cell phone, one girl reading alone by the window, plus the guys behind the counter. Yasmin jumps up from the table and bops around and pretty soon, she's dancing—whirling really. "C'mon!"

I'm shy at first because the two girls sitting together are looking at Yasmin like she's insane, but everyone else is smiling, so I get up and join her and give in to the music. We both dance and then, for some reason, we laugh so hard we're practically crying. I look at Yasmin and realize she *is* crying. But she looks happy. Happy and sad. Both at the same time.

Then an idea pops into my head.

saturday morning

PLANNING COMMITTEE

I call an official meeting of my new *Quinceañera* Planning Committee with Stephanie, Erin, and two tuna and veggie foot-longs from Subway.

We're camped out in Erin's dark blue bedroom full of movie posters, including *Love & Basketball*, *Up*, *Election*, *Space Jam*, and *Juno*. Erin has on sweats, a hoodie, and her basketball sneakers. Her short black hair is uncombed, as usual. Stephanie is wearing a silver dress and silver flats, and her toes sparkle with silver glitter polish. I wonder if she has plans with Jesse later.

I begin. "Here's the thing. I'm taking control of my *quinceañera*, and I need your help."

Erin slaps her hands on her thighs. "I love it!"

"We're in, *la* woman," says Stephanie.

"And you have to promise you'll help me do it MY WAY, even though you don't completely get what this is all about."

Both of them start reacting, like, What does that mean? So I quickly continue.

"I'm not saying it makes tons of sense, but I feel like you guys don't really know what I've been going through with this *quince*, pulled in different directions by my family with these two different cultures and all these expectations."

Stephanie folds her arms in front of her chest. "That's right, because I have NO idea what it's like to be different at school and to have parents who give me speeches every other day about how my sister and I have to work TWICE AS HARD as the other girls because we're black, and we have to do twice as well as my parents did."

Erin chimes in, her cheeks stuffed with tuna, lettuce, and tomato.

"If you cut me, do I not bleed? If you bounce me, do I not dribble?" she asks, quoting really badly from Shakespeare.

"Be serious, Erin."

"Okay," she says. "Try being a Jewish nerd who loves basketball and indie movies and has NO interest in being a doctor or a lawyer, and every time you hear the word Nazi it makes you shiver, like when Stephanie hears the N-word."

"When do I hear the N-word?" asks Stephanie.

"Nylon," Erin whispers.

"Oooh." Stephanie scrunches up her face. "It's true. I HATE nylon."

"Try being the kid," Erin goes on, "whose mother is still freaked out because she once joked when she was ten that she might one day look into marrying a girl."

"What did your mom say?" I ask. Erin's never told us this before. Stephanie and I aren't sure if she's attracted to guys or girls, and we don't dare ask.

"Actually, she was okay with it, until I said the girl wouldn't be Jewish. Ha!"

"But, still," I say, "it's different when your parents aren't born here. I'm not trying to say you guys don't deal with all this other stuff. I just feel like . . . you fit in more with your families."

"Is that why you've been hanging out with Yasmin? And you defended her in that fight?" Stephanie asks. "Because your families both come from Puerto Rico?"

Erin finishes her sandwich in one last huge bite.

"Yasmin is just . . . misunderstood," I tell them.

"Who isn't?" says Stephanie.

"Maybe that's the problem. Maybe everybody feels misunderstood, but nobody talks about it, and it makes us all feel lonely. And the more lonely we feel, the more misunderstood we feel."

Erin and Stephanie just look at each other.

Then I tell them, "Sometimes I'm embarrassed because your parents have fancy jobs and mine don't, and we don't have a lot of money. But my parents work really hard at their jobs, and they don't deserve my being ashamed of what they do."

"Duh," says Erin. "Who cares?"

"What Erin means," clarifies Stephanie, "is we're your friends, and we don't care what your parents do. We just care about you."

"I love you guys." I crush them both in a hug. "Okay," I release them, "enough with the sharing circle. Will you two help me plan this *quinceañera*? I can't do it alone."

Without missing a beat, Erin says, "Only if I can be your

escort. Wait, let me call my mother!"

We all laugh. "Actually, there is someone else I'd like to call," I say.

Forty-five minutes later, Yasmin arrives.

Stephanie and Erin seem uncomfortable when Yasmin walks in. She's wearing a simple blouse and jeans again. I guess she's figured out what she wants to show the world. They all smile and nod at each other, but it's forced.

I tried to explain the rumor situation while we were waiting for Yasmin, but I guess some things you need to figure out for yourself.

"So, what's the first step in *quinceañera* planning?" asks Stephanie.

She uses the full word and pronounces it perfectly. Wow.

"Okay! I need a way for us to make money fast so I can pay for a new party and not put my family in the poorhouse."

"We could sell kisses," suggests Stephanie.

"Gag!" yells Erin.

"No teachers!" says Yasmin. There's an awkward silence. "I mean, I'm allowed to kiss all the teachers I've slept with, of course, but that's it."

Stephanie and Erin are shocked. But then Yasmin and I grin at each other, and finally they grin, too.

"Yasmin," says Stephanie, "we shouldn't have bought into the rumors. I'm really sorry."

"Me, too," adds Erin, "and I don't even care if you are a slut."

"Thanks," says Yasmin. "I think."

"Still, maybe a kissing booth might not be the best thing."

I turn to Erin. "So what's your brilliant alternative?"

"We could sell raffle tickets!"

"What would the winner get?" I ask.

"Kisses!" shouts Stephanie.

"NO!" everybody else shouts back.

"Maybe we could give the winner some Knicks tickets," offers Erin.

"Is that legal?" I ask.

"I don't know, but if it's not and you go to prison, we'll save a bundle on the location for your *quince*."

Erin actually said *quince* and not whatchamacallit!

"What about a stoop sale?" I ask.

"Yeah!" says Erin. "I've got crates and crates of old sports stuff and DVDs I don't watch anymore. My mom would pay me just to get rid of them!"

"I've got shoes and bags and dresses I don't wear," says Stephanie. "Designer stuff, just not my style."

"And I've got all these fancy presents from my *quince* that I never use," adds Yasmin.

"Thank you, guys, that's really cool," I say, writing it all down. "And I have a couple of old skateboards in pretty good condition. Let's talk about locations. Besides prison."

"How about 40/40?" asks Stephanie.

"That's only one of the most expensive clubs in the city. Maybe we can get Jay-Z to sing me happy birthday. What are you smoking?"

"*Cartier*," Stephanie replies in a fake snooty accent. "Just kidding. Sorry."

"Wait, I have an idea! I could ask Iggy, my building

manager, if we could use the community room. It's not the 40/40 Club, but I think it'll work," I say.

Everyone nods. I put Yasmin in charge of decorations. "Maybe you could do some kind of collage?"

"Cool," she says.

Erin offers to film the whole party, which my mother will love.

She grabs her video camera and takes practice shots while we laugh and throw things at her.

The official end of our first planning meeting. Not bad.

It's a good thing we never mailed those invitations.

my new sweet 15

PLAN B

• *I will relax and do my own thing. My new Q will be a small get-together in the community room, where I will put on my emerald green dress (altered my way) with sneakers and dance and eat with friends and family. There will be no* damas *or* chambelanes.

• *I will have a* quinceañera *stoop sale (with the help of Erin, Stephanie, Yasmin, America, and The Jezebels).*

• *I will insist on babysitting (promising to keep my grades up) to cover any and all costs for my Q not covered by the stoop sale.*

• *I will help my parents get back as much of their deposits as possible, which will be a lot cheaper than paying the full amounts. We will nicely cancel the check from Mr. H.*

• *My dad will cook for the party, and we'll plan the menu together. It will include my favorite Puerto Rican dishes: rice and beans,* mofongo, pastilles, *and* arroz con leche *for dessert (rice, milk, and sugar, yum).*

• *Stephanie will provide her speakers and iPod with over 5000 songs and serve as DJ. She promises not to play Beyoncé all night long, and my father will provide the salsa and other old people music.*

• *Erin will shoot my quince and make a DVD.*

• *Using the old invites as new invites, Yasmin will change the location and cut them in the shape of skateboards. She will also handle decorations.*

• *MY new and improved quinceañera will cost a lot less money, time, and stress.*

• *Now all I have to do is convince my family.*

saturday afternoon

THE SHOWDOWN

When I get home from Erin's, my dad is standing outside our building, rubbing his goatee, staring across the street. He's wearing a greasy T-shirt because he's been repairing and cleaning the Pontiac. Nobody else in my neighborhood does that. I go over and say softly, "What are you looking at, Papi?"

He smiles. "Just going down memory lane. You remember what used to be there?"

He points to the construction area on the corner of Columbus Avenue where a bunch of new buildings have risen up.

"A diner?"

"Before that."

"I don't know. I always knew it as a diner," I say.

"It was a candy store, one of those old-fashioned ones where they sold homemade malteds and egg creams. Good people."

"The whole city's changing, huh?"

"Everything changes." He kisses the top of my head.

"Papi, I want to have my *quinceañera*, and I want to help pay for it."

"Ah, *querida*. I told you not to worry about money. You work hard enough in school. If you want a *quinceañera*, we will pay for it."

"I want to do it myself, Papi. I *have* to."

He stares at me for a moment, like I'm not just his little girl. Like he understands.

"Let's talk," he says.

I walk into our building with my father's arm around my shoulder.

When we go in the apartment, my mom's sitting on the sofa with a book, Natasha curled up on her left and my sister curled up with physics homework on her right. A big spread of Chinese takeout is on the coffee table, and a salsa record plays low on the old record player. My mom is reading some Jackie Collins novel. She slips it under a cushion when we walk in, like everybody doesn't know.

"Ooh," I say. "You on the dirty part?"

"My daughters are so mature," Mami declares.

"You're the one hiding books under cushions like Destiny is five," says America, and we all laugh.

After my dad showers, we all dig in and devour the Chinese food while watching the Yankees on TV. As the sun starts to set, I say, "Let's take a walk!"

My mother yawns. "I'm tired, honey."

"I have to go meet up with Hailey and Maritza," says America.

"C'mon," I push. "You can be a little late. It'll be fun. We can go to Zabar's and get some dessert."

My mother shakes her head. "I have a nice coffee cake I bought."

I look at my dad.

"I ate the cake last night," he admits.

"Jon!" My mother clicks her tongue double-time.

My father winks at me.

We head for Zabar's.

"So what's really going on here?" America asks as we walk slowly down Broadway. My dad wisely walks a few paces ahead.

I launch into my speech. "What's going on is that you never ask me what I want. My *quinceañera* wasn't mine. It was yours and Mami's."

"Destiny," says my mother, "I—"

"Mami, you and Papi came here to give us a better life, and you want us to be happy. But you have to let me figure out how to do that for myself. And the same goes for you, America. I know you're trying to teach me everything you've learned. But some things I have to learn on my own."

America opens her mouth, but then she stops and just nods.

"The truth is I'm not really ready to become a woman yet, whatever that means. I'm just turning fifteen, and I have a lot of things to figure out still. So please stop fighting with each other about me. I end up in the middle. And that hurts. It really does! Because I love you both so much."

My mom's lower lip begins to quiver. "I'm a bad mother?"

I put my arm around her. "Of course not."

"Am I a bad sister?" asks America.

"Well . . ." I laugh and put my other arm around her.

"Who is this new Destiny?" demands America.

"I'm just me. I like to ride my skateboard and I think wearing a dress sometimes is okay and I might want a boyfriend someday. I'm not into heels or tiaras or giving away my childhood stuff. And I'm not super religious and I don't want to pretend to be. I want my Sweet Fifteen to be like me."

"I only want you to be happy, Dusty," insists America. "I love you."

"And I love you both," adds my mother. "So does this mean the *quince* is back on?"

"Yes," I tell them.

"But everything Destiny's way! Right, Mami?" says America.

My mother hesitates.

"Please, Mami," I say. "No more secret plans about *caballeros* or anything else."

My mother looks at me and then at my sister. She sighs. "*Sí.*"

"The new plan for my *quinceañera* is to make it cheap and fun."

They both nod silently.

"This lecture is over," I announce. "Time for dessert!"

saturday night

ARE YOU MY CABALLERO?

I knock on the door, and he opens it.

He stands there with a bowl of cereal, the TV on behind him in the living room, wearing a *Dark Knight* T-shirt and shorts.

"*Hola*," says Omar.

"Your doorbell's broken."

"I know."

"Oh."

"My mom's not big on home improvements this week. She's got work early tomorrow so she's sleeping. What're you doing here?" he asks. "Your TV busted again?"

"No, my TV is fine. I think. Actually, I haven't been watching it much lately. But thanks very much for your concern. I'll tell her you asked."

"Cool." He nods nervously.

We stand there in the doorway. I can't tell if he wants me to leave or what.

"Watcha eating?" I ask.

"Sugar Pops. I made them myself."

"Yum."

"Did you know," he continues in one long breath, "that

cereal was once prescribed for all kinds of illnesses and that Corn Flakes were invented accidentally in a hospital when the Kellogg Brothers were trying to make granola and the wheat they were using got stale and they pushed it through these rollers and it came out as a flat, thin flake that they decided to bake?"

"I didn't know."

Then we just stand there some more. Before this whole *quinceañera* business, I never felt uncomfortable with Omar. Never. But now . . .

"Wanna come in?"

I smile. "Sure."

We go into the cluttered living room. Two plastic guitars for Guitar Hero sit in the middle of the room, surrounded by books, a boom box, an exercise bike, and ankle weights. Plants run across the window ledge under a Dominican flag. *Doctor Who* is on TV.

"It's a marathon," he says. "My mom wears earplugs to sleep."

"Sweet."

"Yeah."

So we sit on the sofa and watch TV, and I almost don't want to bring up what happened. Almost.

When the episode we're watching ends, I mute the TV and ask him, "Why did you do the Skate15 thing?"

Omar shrugs.

"Were you jealous of Nicolas? Did you do it to pay me back for ignoring you?"

He shrugs again.

"C'mon, Omar. You have to do better than that. You did an incredibly sneaky and crappy thing, and you made a complete idiot out of me. It was wrong. End of story. Don't ever do anything like that again."

He looks down at his cereal bowl and begins mashing the Sugar Pops with his spoon.

"Did you know I was going to think it was Nicolas? Was that the plan?"

"No, I didn't have a plan. I don't know why I did it. I didn't want to confuse you or anything like that. I guess I thought it would be fun. I mean, I know I'm not Mr. Exciting or anything."

"Is that why you tried to kiss me?"

His face turns a million shades of red.

"I'm not trying to embarrass you. Just don't be silly, okay? You're like my brother."

"But I'm not," he tells me.

"Well, stop trying to be Mr. Exciting. Just be you."

Omar grins. "Deal."

We sit on the sofa, staring at the mute TV screen. I get up. "Okay. I should go."

Omar looks as if he wants to say something, but he doesn't.

I walk toward the door. Then I turn around.

"Will you be my *caballero*?" I blurt out.

"Huh?"

"You heard me."

"Why?"

"Don't ask why."

"Why?"

"Because this is hard enough."

Omar smiles. "Why?"

I smile back. "Because you're stupid."

"Why?"

"Because your mother dropped you on your head."

"Why?"

"Because you kept asking why."

"Why?"

"Because if I'm going to do this Sweet Fifteen thing, I want one of my best friends to be at my side. Will you be my escort?"

Omar stops playing. "Is it because Nicolas turned you down?"

"Nicolas did NOT turn me down. He said he would do it, as a matter of fact."

"So why isn't he?"

I could say a billion things. I could say *I* turned Nicolas down. I could say he just isn't good enough to be my *caballero*. I could say he's completely in love with me, and I don't want to give him the wrong idea!

I go for the truth instead. "He isn't who I thought he was."

"Well, I'm a pretty decent guy."

"Yeah. You are."

"So are you."

I laugh. "I'm a decent guy?"

"You know what I mean."

"What?"

And I think that's the start of another routine but he says, "You're one of the smartest, most fun, most beautiful girls I know."

He says it really quickly, but I hear it all. Now I'm the one blushing.

"So you're my escort? It's official then?"

"Signed. Sealed. Delivered."

"Cool."

"I'll walk you home," he says.

On the way there, I tell him about my new *quince* plans.

"I have an idea," he says. "You could still have a two-part *quinceañera*. But instead of a church, Part One could be outdoors in Central Park. BYOS."

"BYOS?"

"Bring Your Own Skateboard."

"Excellent. Done."

We reach my building.

"Thanks," he tells me.

"No, thank *you* for helping me out."

"Helping you out? C'mon. You're my best friend."

"Well, thanks for being my best friend."

Then Omar grins at me and I swear for the first time, I notice that he has these cute little dimples. Where did they come from?

I realize I'm just staring at him.

Talk about awkward!

So I wave and go inside. Wow! What just happened there? Never find yourself alone with your best male friend who has just become your *caballero*! Strange things can happen.

When I get upstairs, America is busy on the computer.

"Omar is my *caballero*!"

She swivels around on the desk chair, her jaw in her lap.

"What?"

"Yep."

"Well, he should consider himself lucky, that's what I say."

"I'll tell him."

"I never thought this day would come," she declares. "You swear to stay safe no matter what?"

"Yes! Yes! I swear!" I say. "Come on, it's Omar."

"It doesn't matter. You can't leave it up to the boy and—"

"I'm not doing anything!"

"I mean, when it comes to sex—"

"MERRY!"

"It's perfectly normal to think about sex."

"I know, but it's a drag," I say. "It makes things way too complicated, and you find yourself acting like a total moron and saying things like *I like your teeth*."

"Huh?"

"Nothing," I answer quickly.

America joins me on my bed. I put my head in her lap, and she plays with my hair the way she used to when I was little.

"Dusty, you are one of the most mature and stable almost fifteen-year-olds I know, and never forget it. Look what you did with the *Q*. Defying convention. Getting Mami off both of our backs forever."

I look up at her.

"Okay," she says. "Getting Mami off our backs until she decides to plan our weddings."

"Hey, Merry?"

"Yeah?"

"Was the reason you never told Mami about Tomas because you were hoping that you might get back together some day, and you didn't want her to be against him?"

"Maybe . . . something like that. But she knows now."

"His loss," I say.

"Yeah," she agrees. "His loss."

I think about Omar. I wonder if everything between us will become clearer. Maybe I just need to be patient, and the right answer will come. Or, maybe with time, I'll just have to choose. . . .

october 28th

MY Q-DAY

Last night, I could only eat an apple for dinner because my stomach was doing flip-flops. I sat up in bed rereading my favorite book from when I was a kid, *Harriet the Spy,* until I fell asleep. This morning I listen to the Beyoncé, Keisha Cole, Common, Alicia Keyes, Marc Anthony, JLo, and Christina Aguillera iPod mix that Stephanie made to get me in the mood.

Today I turn fifteen for the first and last time in my life.

"Which part is scary and which part is exciting?" Natasha asks me.

I look over at her. She's perched on top of my desk like the lion statues at the 42nd Street library, her front paws draped regally over the edge. Her Highness can always read my mind.

"Well," I say, "what if I forget my little speech or trip or just make a complete dork of myself in general?"

"Don't worry," says Fuzzy, who's lying next to me in bed. "You've been practicing your speech for weeks. If you look like a complete dork, no one can say you didn't try."

"Gee, thanks, Fuzz."

"*De nada,*" replies Fuzzy. "Don't mention it."

"For once I agree with the bear." Natasha yawns, stretches, and jumps off the desk. "The only thing you can do is try and what happens, happens. That's the exciting part, right?"

Natasha is SO smart!

"Right," I say. "It's like one of those improvs in Mr. Porton's class where you're given the situation, but what happens once you're in it could go in a gazillion different directions. That's what today feels like. Whatever direction it goes in, I guess the trick is just to go with it."

"Amen!" Natasha comes over and snuggles next to me on the bed and starts to purr.

"Have you guys been to Issues Group, too?" I ask.

Actually, Issues Group has really helped me to handle things in general. Just talking about things helps. I mean, look at Yasmin and Amanda—they've definitely come a long way. Amanda broke up with Nicolas and while she's not exactly killing me with friendship, she says hi to me in the hallway. And Yasmin began putting up her artwork all over her room, which her mom was seriously NOT happy with at first (it clashes with the décor, she said), but she finally had to admit that her daughter is really talented. Yasmin now dresses the way she wants—sometimes sexy and sometimes not, depending on her mood. And her blue streak is back. So anything's possible for me, too. Anything could happen today. I could fall on my ass or I could find the words to say what I need to say.

On with the show! I go into the kitchen in my PJs. Every inch is filled with boiling, frying, baking pots and pans and trays of food. My mom, America, and I have been helping my dad all week with shopping, chopping, slicing, and dicing, and he's made my favorite breakfast this morning, chocolate chip pancakes.

When my mother sees me, she yells, "Surprise!" and waves

two airplane tickets in the air. She hugs me and America. "The two of you are going to Isabela for Christmas!"

"But you guys can't afford to send us to Puerto Rico," I protest as I sit at the table, where a small space has been cleared off.

My father ruffles my hair. "Because of all your *quinceañera* ideas, we found a little extra. Plus a gift from Julia Hernandez. You know how she feels about young women remembering their roots. I'm sure the two of you are heartbroken that your mami and I can't join you, but you'll have a great time."

"What about the rent being late and the layoffs?" I ask.

"Rent is paid," my father says. "And the union negotiated no layoffs. For now, anyway."

"I love unions," I declare.

"I want to be a union when I grow up," adds America.

My mother squeezes my thigh. "I know my daughters. Admit it, you're dying to go to Isabela!"

She's right. America and I will finally get to see what my parents have been talking about all these years. Isabela, the place where it all began for the Lozada family.

After breakfast, we all dress casual and walk over to Central Park. At the entrance, I get on my skateboard and ride in, at my family's side.

The spot I chose for the first part of my *quince* is under some tall trees near the band shell. I hear some *merengue* trumpets blaring from Omar's boom box. I see Erin and Stephanie and Yasmin and some other friends from school sitting and standing and yapping on benches or rolling around on skateboards, a bustling crowd of jean jackets and windbreakers and backward baseball caps in the cool morning sun. When we come over, they all clap and yell and whistle.

Omar skates up, his green eyes sparkling, and he's holding his board AND a new Plan B Rodriguez Super Future skateboard!

"Wow!" I say as he hands it to me. "Is this from you or my parents?"

"From me. I talked your parents into letting me get it for you a long time ago. I put it together myself."

I hold the board out to him. "I can't take this."

"You'd better." He pushes it back toward me. "I saved my allowance for ten months. I told your mom and dad to keep it secret."

"Well," I say, examining the wheels and the sweet deck, "if you're a good boy, I might let you borrow it. Really, Omar," I kiss him on the cheek, "thank you."

He blushes. "So, you ready?" he asks, pointing. I follow his finger to where he's set up a ramp a few feet away inside the band shell. And I'm scared, because it looks so high. I almost do a Lenny on the spot!

I gulp and nod and jump up into the band shell. I get on the board and roll a bit.

My mother is horrified as she realizes my plan. "Destiny, no!"

"Let her try, Mami," says America.

My father looks at me. "Be careful, *nena!*"

I gulp again and check out the ramp. I can do it. I back up so I have enough distance to make the jump, back, back, back. . . . I can hear Erin and Stephanie and Yasmin shouting "Go, Destiny!" in the distance and other kids cheering as I skate, flying fast, and I GO FOR THE JUMP, hitting the wooden ramp at one end and rolling up and over the other end and my feet stick to the board like glue and I'm in the air, FLYING, and when my wheels finally hit the ground, I'm shaking like jelly.

But I'm still standing!

A few hours later, after having my hair and makeup done *chez* Stephanie, I stand silent and nervous outside the door of the community room, wearing my emerald green dress (which I made short and comfortable) and a pair of matching Converse sneakers.

America comes running toward me. "Grab your phone. You're going to want a picture of this."

But nothing can quite prepare me for the sight of Omar walking down the long hall, sporting my father's old black suit (tailored a bit), a *Wolverine* tie, and shiny black shoes.

"How does he look, Dusty?" asks America.

Omar stares at me.

"He looks good," I mumble.

"You look beautiful," he mumbles back.

Yikes!

Omar and I step into the doorway together. Yasmin has done an amazing job covering the walls with collages of tropical flowers and palm trees, sunbeams and beaches; and the room is ready for dancing, lit with a giant disco ball and covered with *HAPPY QUINCEAÑERA* and *HAPPY BIRTHDAY, DESTINY* balloons.

Two folding tables are stacked high with my father's food and a white and pink frosted cake (with vanilla pudding inside), topped by a doll in skate gear.

Stephanie, Erin, and Yasmin are now wearing dresses while America and her Jezebels are wearing jeans and boots. (It's BYOC, bring your own *caballero* or NOT.) I see lots of blue, pink, lavender, and lilac dresses. I also see some sneakers. Omar's mother is standing near Mrs. H and some of my parents' other friends and coworkers, and Mrs. Diamant is standing with some of the kids in my Issues Group—including Amanda!

There is no religious ceremony. I am escorted into the party by Omar, but I'm NOT followed by my own "court." MY *quinceañera* is NOT about the birthday girl being symbolically escorted into "womanhood" by her family and friends. MY *quinceañera* does NOT look like a wedding. It looks a lot like a party. My BIRTHDAY party.

My father is at the front of the room, dressed immaculately in a dark suit with a striped tie and shiny cufflinks, and my mother's at his side in her wedding pearls, heels, and a red dress. It's like they just stepped out of *Quince Beat*, and I'm glad because it's what they want.

My mother is already crying as Omar and I enter, arm-in-arm. "You look so grown up!" she says.

I waltz with Omar (we practiced with my mom and dad as choreographers). I waltz with my dad. I waltz with my mom. I waltz with America. I waltz with Peter, Hailey's little brother. Then I waltz with Erin and Stephanie and Yasmin and anybody who will have me.

There's a toast by my mom and dad.

Then the time comes for me to read the speech I wrote about what my *quince* means to me. I start by saying that the *quinceañera* (or *quince años* as it's sometimes called, meaning "fifteen years") is a mix of Spanish and Aztec Indian culture that began in the 1500s. At that time, wealthy daughters were sent to a temple to be educated as priestesses. But I'm not a wealthy Mayan or Aztec daughter, and Columbus Prep is no temple.

"For me," I tell them, "becoming a woman is not about trading in my sneakers for high heels or trading in childhood for adulthood or my skateboard for a dress. I think a woman needs all these parts of herself because she's not just one thing. She's not someone put here on this Earth only to be sexy or to serve. She's someone with hopes and dreams of her own, and that could mean getting married and having children, or it could mean something else or it could mean both. She has to try a lot of things before she can find out what she wants."

I read a list of strong Latina women: "Julia de Burgos, poet; Felisa Rincón de Gautier, former mayor of San Juan; María Irene Fornes, playwright; Rosario Ferré, writer; Rita Moreno, Hollywood actress; Chita Rivera, Broadway star; Alicia Alonso, dancer; Celia Cruz, queen of salsa music; Nancy López, champion golfer; Lisa Fernandez, softball pitcher; Lourdes Portillo, filmmaker; Ellen Ochoa, astronaut; Vanessa Torres, champion skateboarder; Sonya Sotomayor, Supreme Court justice; Miriam Lozada, my beloved mother; and America, my beloved older sister."

When I add that America is "not only empowering herself but also reaching out and helping to empower other women," she sniffles worse than my mother!

I end with: "I hope to be like these women one day. And this *quinceañera* is my first step."

I pause and look around as everyone applauds and sings "Happy Birthday" and "*Feliz Cumpleaños*," and I blow out the candles on my pink and white frosted cake, and then America yells, "EVERYBODY DANCE NOW!" and everyone starts dancing.

My father comes over and asks, "So? How does it feel to be fifteen?"

"It's pretty good so far."

He kisses both my cheeks. "If you're happy, I'm happy."

"You should ask Mami to dance."

"You think?"

"Yeah, I do."

"She's a little mad at me for letting you make that skateboard jump."

I nudge him toward my mother, who is standing in a corner by the punch bowl table, receiving guests. They congratulate her as if she's just won *la lotería*. My dad holds out his hand, my mom takes it, and they dance a hot and smoking *tango*. I don't mind. I'm kind of proud even. Soon, everyone on the dance floor is doing the *tango*. Or almost doing the *tango*.

I realize my birthday is almost over.

I look at Omar, and he makes a funny duck noise at me. I go over to him and he takes my hand and we dance, too. America dims the lights and I imagine that we're in a fancy ballroom. At one point, Omar moves really close to me, and I don't move away. I don't think it makes me a Stupid Girl if I might like spending more time with Omar. I mean, he wears *Incredible Hulk* socks and he laughs too loud after he's said something nerdy and he's not the world's best dancer and steps on my feet about six hundred times, but underneath all that Omar's . . . even more quirky and I bet there are a lot more cute quirks waiting to come out. Omar's not a boy. He's an adventure!

"What're you thinking about?" he whispers.

"Nothing."

"We don't have to keep dancing."

"That's okay," I whisper. "It's kind of fun."

When we finally break, my hands are all sweaty and my heart's pounding a little. Pounding for Omar!

The music changes and Omar asks, "Should we practice some more?"

"Definitely. We should."

And in the community room, with everyone watching, we dance and dance and dance.

He beams and there go those little dimples again and I kiss his cheek and he kisses mine. Then I do it. I kiss him on the lips. It's a quick kiss, but we know. I make a funny duck noise at him, and then we join our friends and family in a big dance.

My legs are still longer than the rest of me, but I don't care. I'm tall and I like my legs. They're mine. And they look pretty good in this dress. I kick off my sneakers, and I use my legs to do the *tango*. And the *mambo*. And the *salsa,* the *merengue,* the *bachata*, the *plena*, the *bomba*, and the *rumba.* The funky chicken and the electric slide. *My* version of them, anyway.

I swing. I clap. I stomp. I shake. I wiggle. I twist. I turn. I dance.

I dance with everybody and everything. Without shame. Without fear. Without judgment. I dance.

(For one night, at least.)

And I am grateful. . . .

Gratitud.

The End . . . I hope . . . for now. . . .